He didn't know where he was going.

If he was going . . . how he was going. Some force outside of himself seemed to be controlling him. It wasn't what R.J. said. He hadn't gone soft on that girl.

Yet, when he closed his eyes, why couldn't he see anything else? Why, when he awakened, did his thoughts immediately center on her? Why did he feel the need to continue to protect her?

Each day he watched her as if mesmerized. He found himself looking at her like a starving man gazing at a feast that he was not invited to eat. His eyes would follow the familiarity of her every gesture, the sweetness of her smile.

He remembered kissing her. He remembered their quick passion. . . .

Why was he still here? he asked himself.

Instinctively he knew the answer, but he shied away from admitting it.

Dear Reader:

*We at Silhouette are very excited to bring you a NEW reading **Sensation**. Look out for the four books which will appear in our new Silhouette **Sensation** series every month. These stories will have the high quality you have come to expect from Silhouette, and their varied and provocative plots will encourage you to explore the wonder of falling in love – again and again!*

Emotions run high in these drama-filled novels. Greater sensual detail and an extra edge of realism intensify the hero and heroine's relationship so that you cannot help but be caught up in their every change of mood.

*We hope you enjoy this new **Sensation** – and will go on to enjoy many more.*

We would love to hear your comments about our new line and encourage you to write to us:

Jane Nicholls
Silhouette Books
PO Box 236
Thornton Road
Croydon
Surrey
CR9 3RU

GINGER CHAMBERS
Firefly in the Night

Silhouette Sensation

First published in Great Britain in 1989
by Silhouette Books, Eton House, 18–24 Paradise Road,
Richmond, Surrey TW9 1SR

© Ginger Chambers 1988

Silhouette, Silhouette Sensation and Colophon are
Trade Marks of Harlequin Enterprises B.V.

ISBN 0 373 57490 8

18–8902

Made and printed in Great Britain

Chapter One

Cord Anderson sat with his back to the wall, arms crossed lightly over his chest, narrowed eyes not missing a movement in the cavernous lobby as businessmen and women, dressed in suits and clutching briefcases, flowed into the building like lemmings. With a deceptive air of aloof detachment, he studied the tightness reflected in their features, the taut way they held their bodies, the intentness of their minds. Like modern gladiators, they were off to do battle with telephone and computer and each seemed just as unsure as those in ancient days of who the victor might be. Once, he might have been one of them if he had chosen another course, followed a different path. But he had done neither of those things, and for good or bad, he couldn't say that he was sorry.

One long jeans-clad leg became cramped from too long a time in inactivity and he shifted it. His action drew the attention of a nearby security guard. When the man's mouth tightened with automatic disapproval, Cord pretended not to notice him. He wasn't here to please the man. He wasn't here to please any man—not even the one who had summoned him.

The muted ring of a telephone was soon followed by the guard motioning for Cord to come to the security station. With indolent ease, Cord rose from the bank of chairs, unfolding his lean length until he had reached his full six foot two inches.

"Mr. Richards can see you now. Sign this," the guard said, tapping a notebook with numbered lines that was lying on top of his desk. Cord added his name under the name of the last visitor from yesterday. "Wear this at all times while you're in the building," the guard continued in a stiff tone as he thrust a plastic visitor's badge beside the notebook. "And don't forget to give it back when you're done. Mr. Richards's secretary will be down shortly to accompany you to his office."

"Thanks," Cord murmured. As he picked up the badge, his cool gray eyes flickered over the man across from him. Cord had seen his type before: men puffed up by the importance of their uniform but of doubtful help when a real emergency threatened.

He clipped the badge to the pocket flap of his faded denim jacket. He had come straight from the airport, not having had either the time or the inclination to change.

A few of the people passing by glanced at him, his appearance breaking their concentration. Their eyes, especially those of the women, swept over him with surprised interest.

Cord resettled in his chair. At his feet, stuffed in the space of a worn duffel bag, sat most of his worldly possessions. He was prepared to wait for as long as it took.

Soon a woman appeared at his side. "Mr. Anderson?" she questioned, her tone brisk. When he nodded, she said, "Come with me, please."

Cord reached for his bag.

"You'll have to leave that here with me," the security man called, starting around his desk.

"I don't think so," Cord said softly, a warning lurking behind his words.

The guard's face flushed. "It's the rule," he bleated.

Cord's hand tightened on the duffel bag's strap, his darkly handsome features not giving away any of his thoughts.

"It's all right, Waldo," the secretary intervened. "He can bring the bag."

"But—"

The secretary motioned to Cord. "This way."

As Cord followed her, he could feel the guard's impotent gaze burning into his back. But since he had suffered much worse during his lifetime, a simple hard look meant nothing to him.

The journey in the elevator to the twenty-second floor was silent. The secretary, embroiled in her own thoughts, left Cord to his.

A few years back he never would have considered doing a job of this kind, not even for an old friend of his father's. But then a few years back he had been younger—forty had not been staring him quite so closely in the face. His bones hadn't started to ache occasionally from old wounds, his mind hadn't begun to question the futility of his actions.

The elevator doors whooshed open and they stepped into a long corridor that led to the reception area of a suite of executive offices. The secretary disappeared through the first doorway to the right and held the door open for him to follow.

"Mr. Richards's office," she said, motioning across the wide expanse of carpeting.

Cord nodded shortly and moved to the interior door. He opened it without notification. A man was seated behind an expansive mahogany desk. Behind his back was a bird's-eye view of the city of Houston. Green clusters of trees were cut by ribbons of cement and steel. Freeways spread into the suburbs.

The man rose to his feet and extended his hand. Cord took it after a moment's hesitation. He had met the man only once before, after one of his father's questionable business deals had landed him in trouble with the law. Cord had been a teenager then, ready to graduate from high school. The man had come to the small town where his father reigned supreme and saved him from a jail sentence at worst and a financially strapping fine at best. The man had aged a great deal over the intervening years: his dark blond hair had changed to silver, wrinkles had softened his eaglelike look, but his dark eyes remained the same— alert, intelligent, quick to spot a flaw in any line of reasoning.

"Cord! I'm glad you could come. Sit down."

Cord took the proffered chair. He felt the man's gaze run assessingly over him. He met the look with level calm. He had nothing to hide.

"You're the spitting image of your father at your age," William Richards said as he retook his seat. "You're what? Thirty-seven, thirty-eight?"

Cord nodded. He saw no reason to settle on the latter.

The older man leaned back in his chair. "Your father and I had some good times when we were young. A regular pair of rapscallions. Has he ever told you about any of our adventures?"

"No. Never."

William Richards ignored the quiet reply. He seemed intent on reminiscing. A fond smile had settled on his features. "The things we used to do. Drove my father almost crazy, not to mention your grandparents." He shook his head. "Had some tight scrapes."

After a silent moment while Cord remained perfectly still, the man recalled himself to the purpose of the meeting. He sat forward and folded his hands on his desk, his face losing all traces of warmth.

"Did your father mention why I wanted to see you?"

"He gave me a brief summary."

"Then you understand the seriousness of the situation."

Cord nodded.

The man's hands tightened convulsively. Cord's eyes flickered to the telltale sign of agitation and then back to the man's face. "If there were any other way around this," William Richards continued, "I'd use it. But I don't see any."

"Wouldn't a simple warning work?" Cord asked.

The man laughed shortly. "If you knew the girl like I do.... No, a warning wouldn't have any effect on her. In fact, it might make the situation worse."

"And that's something you want to avoid at any cost."

"I'm willing to pay whatever it takes."

"Then I guess that's why you can afford me."

"You don't come cheap."

Cord's smile wasn't pleasant. "No, I don't."

The man's eyes narrowed. "But you *will* get the job done. I have to know that. I won't pay a penny unless—"

"I'll get it done," Cord interrupted. He shifted position. "But I'm not sure I agree with the method you want me to use to snatch her. It's too loose-ended. Someone might see."

"We'll have to take that chance."

"Will you agree to let me refine it? It's the only way I'll do it."

The man's dark eyes held Cord's steady gaze. Cord could see the desperation in their depths.

Finally William Richards gave a tight nod. "What's your idea?" he asked. Cord's explanation was succinct. When he finished, the older man gave his reluctant approval. Then, sliding open a side drawer of his desk, he reached inside.

Cord tensed, an automatic reaction. He relaxed only when he saw the man extract a clipping from a magazine.

"Here," William Richards said, handing it across to him. "This was taken a year or so ago at some kind of charity function, but she still looks about the same."

Cord turned the clipping around so that he could see it and he soon found himself looking into a pair of widely spaced eyes that were a light, guileless blue. Her hair was a pale wheat color that fell to her shoulders in a soft line; her face was delicately formed with eyebrows that winged upward.

Again he wondered if he should turn the job down. This was so far removed from his usual fare. Then he remembered the weariness he had been carrying like a weight on his shoulders for the past six months. He thought of the nights of disturbed sleep where he would awaken with a cold chill, the days when haunted memory would give him no peace. Causes no longer interested him. They all came down to greed. Greed for power, greed for wealth. At the moment he wanted no more of it.

"May I keep this?" he asked, flicking a corner of the clipping with his thumb.

"Of course."

"You have everything else arranged?"

"Yes." He told Cord of his plans.

Cord nodded. "That sounds all right, but I'll check it out."

"I thought you might," William Richards murmured.

Cord pushed to his feet. He didn't extend his hand to seal the agreement. "I'll be in touch," he said.

The older man nodded tightly.

HE MOVED QUIETLY across the lobby, his steps like those of a leopard on the prowl. He arrived at the security desk without the guard noting his approach. With one flick of his wrist, he deposited the plastic badge onto the teak surface. The security guard jumped as if he had been shot.

Cord's gray eyes met his startled look. Then, without a word, he turned on his heels and walked away, leaving the man to stare after him.

The guard watched as the visitor pushed through one of the heavy glass doors and strode into the oppressive heat of a Houston summer morning. His eyes continued to follow the tall, spare form for as long as the glass wall allowed. Then a shiver started at the base of the man's spine and ran full length up his back. He had read descriptions of people with danger written on their faces in some of the men's action magazines he collected. He had even practiced giving such looks in his bathroom mirror. But if this experience was what it was like to come into contact with someone who actually wore that look, he hoped never to see it again.

Chapter Two

Marlie hurried along the sidewalk, trying to control the urge to look over her shoulder. Her body felt stiff, tight, even as her heart beat in double time. Her footsteps sounded loud in her ears—a quick tattoo against the pavement. Surely nothing could happen to her here. Not on campus, not at midday, not in full view of everyone.

She gave in to the need to glance around and then quickly snapped her head forward again. He was still there. Following behind her, some twenty yards away. Other students were between them, laughing and talking, concerned only with their next class or with what they were going to do later that afternoon. But she could see him, just as he could see her. She felt his eyes burning into her.

Marlie continued walking. Her first instinct was to run, but where? Her books grew heavy in her arms; her neck began to hurt from tension. If only someone she knew would walk by!

She needed to stay in a crowd. The wrong thing to do would be to isolate herself.

She glanced over her shoulder again, unable to stop herself. Her head bobbed, trying to peer around the people in the path, but more students had joined the procession behind her, blocking her view.

The central library building was just ahead. Her footsteps quickened. She mounted several steps and then turned, hanging tightly onto the railing. She watched as the students moved by.

He wasn't there! Her head swiveled, her eyes darting in all directions. She began to tremble. Just as had happened twice before in the past few days, he had disappeared as if in a puff of smoke. One moment he was there, menacing her, the next he was not.

Marlie sank slowly to the step, her legs no longer offering support. Who was he? Why was he following her? She pushed her light blond hair away from her face. Was she going crazy, or what? No, she assured herself, she wasn't. He had been there, just as he had before.

Was he trying to frighten her? Was that it? But that made as little sense as anything else.

A shoe scraped on a nearby step and Marlie jumped defensively. Her gaze flew to the person who had come to stand next to her. She braced herself, ready to attack if the need arose.

She looked up into the smiling face of one of her fellow students. Mark Herron's bright red hair was gleaming in the sun, his comfortable features arranged expectantly.

"Are you skipping class?" he asked. "If you are, may I come along? An afternoon with you would be much more interesting than an hour spent with Old Man Tucker."

The relief Marlie felt was almost debilitating. She struggled to her feet, trying to return his smile. "No, I was just... I'm going to class. I have a paper to turn in."

"My tough luck," her friend replied.

He took her arm and they started to move away, descending the steps and then turning onto the pathway. Marlie used the time to look around. There was still no sign of the man. When would she see him again? Later today? Tonight? Tomorrow morning? And would he continue to disappear? Or would he come forward to do...what? She shied away from the answer, knowing that soon she would have to come to some sort of decision. Matters could not continue as they were.

"Is he still out there?" a hushed feminine voice asked from close behind her shoulder.

"I don't know. I can't see him anymore."

"Who *is* he?"

Marlie let the blind slat snap back into place before moving to sit in one of the matching chairs that faced an impressive stone fireplace. In summer, cut wood and grate were replaced by a colorful spray of dried flowers, which made the room as cheerful in that season as a crackling fire did in winter. Her reflective gaze centered on the flowers for a moment before shifting to her friend, who had taken her place at the window.

"I don't know that, either. I just know that he's been following me for the past few days."

"He follows you everywhere?" Regina Campo asked. When she turned, her eyes were wide in her round face.

Marlie shrugged. "I don't know. But he's there a lot. And when he's not, it's as if I can still *feel* him."

Regina's dark eyes began to gleam with amusement. "Maybe he's a spy!"

"Don't be silly."

"Or maybe he's someone who's so impressed with your combination of beauty and brains that he just can't leave you alone. He wants to be near you, even if from afar."

"You're getting sillier."

Regina laughed. "That comes from being around my mother for too long. I love her; I truly do. It's just that she starts to drive me wild after a few days. The way she acts, she still thinks I'm a child. Do this, do that...don't forget to... It's a wonder she doesn't come in to check that I've brushed my teeth before I go to bed at night. I think this little visit is going to have to come to an end pretty soon."

"Your mother's a very nice person," Marlie defended. "She's just trying to make you feel loved."

"Oh, I know. I know. And everyone tells me I'm just like her. But maybe it's because we *are* so much alike that we can't live together. And being an only child doesn't make it any easier. She concentrates all her attention on me. There's no one else to dilute all that mother love."

"Appreciate her," Marlie advised soberly.

Regina suddenly lost her smile. "Oh, Marlie, I'm sorry. I didn't mean—"

"It's all right. You haven't. I'm okay."

Regina still looked pained. "I'm such a dolt sometimes. I know how much you miss your mother. I was so sorry to hear... I wish I could have come back to the States to be with you." When Marlie said nothing, she took a breath and continued, "I do appreciate my mother. I really do. And I probably drive her just as wild as she does me. But it's a nice sort of wild. I'd miss her terribly if..."

When her friend's voice trailed away, Marlie said softly, "I know."

Regina's gaze was apologetic. She glanced at the window and motioned outside. "Are you frightened about this man who's following you?"

"A bit," Marlie answered, not giving the full truth. "But I'm curious, too. I don't understand why he's doing it."

"So what are you going to do?"

Marlie shrugged.

Regina claimed the chair opposite her. "Do you think this could be something serious? Something you should tell the police about?"

"They'd think I was just another crazy seeing things."

"They wouldn't!"

"They would."

The two women sat in silence for a time. Then, abruptly, Marlie stood up.

"What are you doing?" Regina asked. She was alarmed by the way Marlie's mouth had set into a determined line. She knew that look from old, and knew that her friend didn't always consider the consequences of what she chose to do.

"I'm going to find out for myself," Marlie answered.

"What do you mean?"

"I'm going to find the man and ask him why he's following me."

Regina stared at her blankly. "You're going to what?"

"I'm going to find him and ask him why he's following me," she repeated patiently.

Regina sprang to her feet. "No, Marlie, don't. That's not a good idea."

"Do you have a better suggestion?"

"But he might be dangerous!"

"I doubt it." That wasn't entirely the truth. Remembered fear shuddered through her. But the situation couldn't continue as it had and this was the only way she knew to resolve it.

"I still think you should call the police."

"And say what? 'Officer, please help me. I think someone is following me!' "

"That would be the intelligent thing to do."

"I want this to stop, Regina. And the only way I can see to make it stop is to confront him."

Regina looked steadily into Marlie's blue eyes, seeing her firm resolve. Finally she said, "Then at least let me come with you. Safety in numbers and all that."

Marlie smiled. She and Regina had been best friends for the past twenty-one years, since the time each was five and Regina's family had moved into the house next door to the one Marlie lived in in the quiet, exclusive area of Houston's near west side. That was a lot of years, a lot of shared experiences. They were as close as sisters.

"All right. If you insist."

"I insist."

Almost instantly a look of apprehension settled on Regina's face as she realized just what she had committed herself to. But it disappeared under Marlie's teasing appraisal.

They crossed the front threshold one after the other and paused under the narrow portico. The last time Marlie had seen the man was before she had hurried into Regina's house. He must have followed her from the university because he had been sitting in a dark blue sedan parked next to the curb a short distance along the street. The car was gone now, but Marlie still had the feeling that he was there, somewhere, watching her.

"Come on," she said. "Let's look farther down the street."

"You don't see him?" Regina was unable to hide her relief.

"No." Marlie moved down the pathway toward the sidewalk. When she felt the close distance her friend was keeping to her back, she experienced a fond feeling of déjà vu. Through all the years of their childhood, this was the way it had been. She had always gotten them into whatever scrapes had occurred, with Regina, a much more placid soul, invariably taking a less-than-willing part. Not that she, herself, was fearless. In reality she was apprehensive about many things, but she tried not to let it show. As a child, possibly it was because she was sensitive to the fact that she was adopted and she didn't want to disappoint her new parents; as an adult, possibly it was habit. She didn't know. She was preparing for a master's degree in history, not psychology. All the same, she didn't like to be afraid, or act afraid. Such behavior wasn't acceptable to her.

They stopped at the sidewalk to study the street in each direction. No one was there who shouldn't be. A yardman, several houses to the right, was busy blowing grass clippings away from the edge of a driveway with one of those horrible blowers that make so much noise. A utility services person was assisting someone in the depths of a manhole in the street to the left. There was no dark blue sedan or suspicious man.

Marlie gave an impatient sigh. "He's not here."

"Don't sound so disappointed," Regina urged.

"That doesn't mean he won't be back."

"No...Marlie, promise me you won't do anything stupid."

"I won't," she promised lightly.

Regina touched her arm. "No, I mean it! Don't do anything that will get you into trouble. You don't know who this man is...what his reasons are."

"If I talk to him, I'll be able to find out, won't I?"

"I don't want to read about you in the newspaper, Marlie."

"On the feature page?" Marlie teased.

"In the obituaries." Regina's face was so serious that Marlie broke into laughter, and soon Regina relaxed enough to laugh as well. "That might be an exaggeration," she conceded. "But not by that much. You will be careful, won't you?"

"I'll be careful."

"You know, if you turn up missing or anything, I'll never forgive you."

Marlie leaned forward to press her cheek lightly against her friend's. "I know," she said. "But don't worry. Nothing is going to happen to me."

Until the week before, the two friends had not seen each other in eighteen months. Regina had gone to Italy to stay with some relatives to further her studies of Renaissance art. But upon her return, their relationship had taken up immediately where it had left off.

"Would you like that cup of tea now?" Regina asked. "We never did have a chance to get it."

Marlie consulted her watch. "No, I'd better not. Dad will be home soon."

Her friend nodded understanding. There was no need for Marlie to explain that she liked to be present when her father arrived home. Over the past year, since her mother's unexpected death, she had tried in as many ways as she could to take some of the hollowness from her father's eyes. Each evening Monica had been at the door to greet her husband with a dry martini and a calm loving ear to listen to his tribulations of the day. So Marlie had taken up the cause, even to the point of moving back home from the apartment that she loved. But she loved her father more. She would do anything for him.

The two friends parted and as Marlie walked the short distance back to her home, she inspected it with a discerning eye. It looked the same as all the other houses that surrounded it: a spacious, scrupulously landscaped yard that housed a multistoried dwelling with an impressive facade. But to her, this particular house always had been special. From the day of her arrival when she was three, she retained a vivid impression that the house had smiled at her. And possibly it had, because she had been made welcome there and given love.

Marlie paused to send another quick glance around before letting herself in the front door. The only addition to the scene of a few minutes before was a dog, prancing happily on its leash, in the care of its owner. No car. No man.

Thoughtfully, she stepped into the entryway. Should she call the police as Regina suggested? But exactly what would she say in order not to sound like an idiot? The police probably had crackpots calling all the time with stories of paranoia. But if she did keep silent and something did happen . . .

Marlie shook her head in dismissal. No, nothing would happen. If the man had wanted to kidnap her—or worse—he'd had ample opportunity to do so. And he had not. So his presence was purely a nuisance. At least, she tried to convince herself that this was so.

She had withheld telling her father because for the past week he had seemed unusually distracted. Something was worrying him and she hadn't wanted to add to his burden. But possibly tonight she would casually mention the man to him and see what he would advise. Not that she was incapable of handling the situation herself. She could. She was an adult. It was just that the man's continuing presence bothered her. And if her father had any ideas that might help, she would listen to him.

MARLIE LOWERED THE SECTION of newspaper she was reading to look at her father. Some minutes earlier he had appropriated the business section, professing an interest in a new company that was being formed in the city. Yet now he was sitting with the paper forgotten, his gaze fixed blankly on one book-lined wall. The study was a cozy place, smelling faintly of good cigars and well-cared-for leather. It had always been Marlie's favorite room, possibly because her father had never barred her entry. Many evenings during her childhood years she had played quietly on the richly designed Oriental carpet while her father had sat at his desk and prepared briefs for upcoming cases.

Marlie put her section of newspaper away, no longer feeling the need to camouflage her thoughts. She moved to her father's side and gently slid the paper from his unresisting fingers. He blinked, surprised by the action, unnerved by his own inattentiveness.

"What are you doing?" he asked. The angles of his features were starkly outlined and he held himself with uncharacteristic tenseness.

Marlie balanced herself on one arm of the chair and leaned close to hug his neck.

"Getting your attention," she answered.

Her father made a gruff noise deep in his throat and tried to retrieve his newspaper. "I was reading that."

"No, you weren't," she contradicted.

His dark eyes met her lighter ones and he smiled slightly before admitting, "I guess you're right."

Marlie examined his tired face. "What is it, Dad? What's bothering you? I know something is."

"It's nothing," he said. He pushed to his feet and walked stiffly to the small rosewood desk that fitted in perfectly with the room. Once there, he reached for a miniature skier balanced precariously on a round metal base and began to toy with it, forcing the skier to rock back and forth. The desk toy and others of its kind had been the rage when Marlie was younger and she had given it to her father as a gift.

Marlie moved to stand beside him. "Won't you tell me about it?" she persisted. "Maybe telling me will help."

He gave the skier another disturbing nudge before turning to face her. By now he had forced most of the strain from his features and he was wearing the confident look he affected when in front of a jury. "I've told you, it's nothing." But when he sensed her continuing doubt, he shrugged and said, "Just a little problem at the office, that's all. Nothing for you to worry about."

Marlie placed a hand on her father's arm. She felt the slight tremor he gave.

His eyes wandered over her face and something in them—a flash of regret?—caused her heart to start beating more strongly. Something was wrong. Something definitely was wrong.

"Dad—" she started to say when he interrupted her.

"How was your day? Did the car give you any more trouble?"

"No," she answered shortly, not wanting to be distracted.

"I've always loved sports cars," her father mused. "I had an MG-TD when I was younger. Looked great, ran horribly. I was forever having to put it in the shop to be fixed. And I can tell you, on the income I had at the time, that car kept me broke. Still, I hated to see it go when I was finally forced to sell it. But then I got a..."

Marlie listened while her father talked. Even under the circumstances, she loved to hear him speak. He had one of those wonderful rich voices that seduce a person's ear. That, coupled with his quick, intelligent mind, made him a perfect lawyer. Only today, she had the definite suspicion that he was playing for time. He didn't want to confide what was bothering him. He didn't want to be questioned. He patted her hand when he finished and she felt the quick glance he gave that gauged his success in distracting her.

Marlie's eyes dropped to the picture of her mother, which still held place of pride on his desk. She wished that Monica would sweep into the room as she used to, bringing radiance and warmth, and making all their problems—major or minor—disappear with the sweetness of her smile.

Her father, following the line of her vision, questioned gruffly, "You miss her, don't you?"

Marlie nodded.

"I do, too," he said. He was silent a moment before he asked, "Do you trust me, honey?"

Marlie looked at him in surprise. "Yes, of course I do."

"And do you realize that every decision I make is one that I've weighed heavily? And that when it concerns you, I've weighed it even more?"

Marlie's eyes were troubled. "Yes, but—"

Her father held up a silencing hand. "I just want you to remember that, that's all."

"I will. Dad, you're frightening me."

His smile softened the gravity of his features. "I wouldn't want to do that. No matter how much you've grown, I still remember you as that tiny little girl who came into my life and turned it upside down. Blond hair, big blue eyes and such a serious little face.''

''I remember the first time I saw you, too. You opened up your arms and I ran into them.''

''It took a little coaxing,'' he said, chuckling. ''You just don't remember that part.''

''I love you, Dad.''

''And I love you—maybe more than you know.''

Again Marlie searched his face, hoping for a sign that would tell her what he was thinking. But once again he had reverted to what she termed his trial face, letting nothing show.

''I'm tired, sweetheart. I think I'm going to go to bed early tonight.''

Marlie experienced a sudden chill of apprehension as her father started to move away from her. ''Dad... You aren't ill, are you? I mean, you wouldn't hide something like that from me, would you?''

He didn't smile as he turned to look at her. ''No, honey, I wouldn't,'' he said. Then he left the room.

Once she was alone, Marlie reached for Monica's picture and hugged it to her breast. If only her mother were still here. She would know what to do, what to say.

THE SMALL RED SPORTS CAR backed to the end of the long driveway with practiced precision. Marlie checked the street for traffic and, seeing none, continued on her way, backing the car and then shifting it forward. She was late for class. Somehow her alarm clock hadn't rung at its usual time and she had showered and donned her clothing in record time.

She had been surprised to find her father in the kitchen. Usually he left for the office long before she made an appearance. But when she thought about it, she decided that he probably had risen late as well. Some sort of electrical problem in the night must have thrown them both off schedule.

She had reached for the coffee cup he offered, swallowed a piece of toast practically whole and started for the door. But her father had gotten there first. In fact, he had blocked her way. And when she looked up at him in confusion, he'd drawn her roughly into his arms and given her a great bear hug before pushing her away. She would have sworn that his eyes were misty, but he didn't give her time to examine him closely. He was busy cautioning her not to drive too fast—his usual admonishment when she was in a hurry—and with that common, everyday repetition he had propelled her on her way.

Marlie whipped the small car around a series of corners to gain a busy commuter street. As usual, traffic was terrible. Cars crept along, engines humming, drivers' tempers growing short. Marlie suffered with it until she reached the street that was her short-cut. The beauty of it was that it ran through a residential section that few others of the teeming mob trying to travel from one section of the city to the other had discovered. Her father, bless him, had shown her this route himself. One of his business associates lived in the area so he knew it quite well. The streets were practically empty, with most of the residents just waking up to the new day. Marlie shook her blond hair, enjoying the feeling of the wind tossing it this way and that. Huge pine trees mottled the rays of the sun. And for the first time in what seemed to be ages, her spirits lifted and she reveled in the simple fact that she was alive. Today she had yet to see the man who had been following her. Maybe he *was* a figment of her imagination or it all was a strange coincidence. And possibly her father's problem *was* something at the office that would cause them no harm. Anyway, the morning was too beautiful for her to dwell on negative thoughts. Just for this time, for this short space of minutes, she wasn't going to let herself worry about anything. The sun, when it broke through the shading clusters of pine needles, was warm on her face, the radio station was playing a song that she liked, and all was temporarily right with her world.

Marlie hummed along with the contagious beat of the music. But as she turned onto yet another street in the quiet district, the sight that greeted her caused her musical accompaniment to dry on her lips. A short distance away a white van was slewed at an odd angle across the lane, its cargo doors thrown open. Automatically, Marlie's foot lifted from the accelerator, causing the sports car to slow to a crawl as she neared the van. A tall man was standing at the rear of the van. He stepped forward and waved a beseeching hand.

Marlie's first instinct was to whip around the obstacle. As it was, she was already going to be late for her first class. She didn't need any further delay. But the man waved to her again. He needed assistance. She braked the car to a complete stop and smiled inquiringly at him as he approached. Consciously, she registered his dark good looks and air of steely fitness even as she asked, "Is there something I can do to help?"

The man was dressed in a workman's uniform of khaki-colored slacks and matching shirt, yet there was no insignia on either of his pockets or on the van.

"Yeah," he replied. His voice was low, quiet. "I seem to have picked up a little trouble."

Marlie frowned. Her car's engine was still running. She glanced at her watch. "What kind of trouble?"

"It's in the back of the van." He motioned to the open doors.

"What is it?"

"A dog. It ran out into the street in front of me and I hit it. I was going to take it to a vet but I think it might need some help now and I don't know what to do for it."

Marlie's fingers were already shutting off the ignition key before the man had finished speaking. He stepped back as she opened her door to get out. Animals were one of Marlie's soft spots. Regina had often teased her by saying that she was a one-woman crusade for anything soft and furry. Throughout her childhood the house had been filled with a procession of pets, from stray cats and dogs to a raccoon that had gotten one of its feet caught in a trap and had to live out its life functioning on the remaining three. Since she was adopted, Marlie could see no reason not to adopt herself, and her doting parents had indulged her.

"How bad is it?" she asked, hurrying toward the van.

"Pretty bad," the man said from close behind her.

Marlie stopped at the doors. She glanced at the man's strongly carved features and then turned back, bracing herself for what she was about to see. Her perfect morning had disappeared instantly, but then the animal's had ended up worse.

When she leaned inside, the interior gloom caused her to blink as she tried to adjust her eyes from the brightness of day.

"I don't..." she started to say when the next thing she knew, large hands were circling her waist and she felt herself lifted. With more force than finesse, she was tossed onto something soft and the doors were slammed shut behind her.

For a moment, all Marlie could do was stare in shock. She heard one of the front doors of the van open and close and the engine sprang to life. Then they were moving.

She took a deep breath. He had thrown her into the van. There was no dog. The dog was a ploy. A ploy to...

She was being kidnapped!

Marlie scrambled to the rear doors, her fingers groping in the half light for a handle, anything to release the barrier so that she could be free. But there was none. Where the handle should have been, there was a space.

Marlie's heart was thundering in her ears. Her breath was coming rapidly. Like a trapped animal, she let instinct guide her and she crawled quickly to the front of the cargo area. If she couldn't get out the back, she would get out the front. She was not going to stay here. But at the front, a good two feet from the driver's seat, a wire mesh stopped her progress. She pushed against it; she rattled it, her fingers wrapping through the tiny holes. But her efforts did no good. Finally, she threw her weight against it repeatedly, hoping to dislodge it. But it held firm. She looked helplessly at the sides of the van—there were no windows.

"My advice is to just sit still," the man offered levelly.

His voice came as a shock to her. Her eyes flew to him, wild, panic-stricken. Then a slowly building anger burst forth.

"Let me out of here!" she charged.

The man laughed. "After all the trouble I went to to get you? No, I don't think so."

"Who are you?" she demanded.

The man remained silent.

"Why are you doing this?" Her mind raced. What could his reason be? Why would anyone want to kidnap her? She thought of Regina's worried comments yesterday and her own amused reaction and she couldn't believe that her fears had actually come true.

This had to be a dream. It couldn't be happening to her. She was still at home, in her bed, asleep. She would wake up in a few minutes—she always did wake up from nightmares. And she would sit up to look at the white, mint-green and coral accessories of her room and she would laugh. Shakily, but she would laugh. Then she would find her father and laugh with him as she told him about the man who had been following her and how she had wondered if—

Her head whirled around to the man in the driver's seat. All she could see of him was the back of his dark head and the tan material that covered his shoulders.

He wasn't the same man. That man had been much shorter, and much less nice-looking. But could he be an accomplice?

Marlie's fingers wove back through the tightly drawn wire. She clung to it. This was no dream. She was awake, she was here. She could feel the vibration of the van's engine and the road slipping by beneath her.

"Please—" She tried again. "I don't know why you're doing this, but I—"

"Just sit back and stop worrying."

"How can you say that?" she cried. Tears of frustration and fear welled up in her eyes. She wiped them brusquely away with the tips of her fingers. She was not going to cry. And she was not going to accept this mildly, no matter what the man thought. He had shown no weapon yet. He hadn't needed to. Marlie cursed herself for her vulnerability.

She rattled the wire vigorously. "I want out of here!"

The man said nothing, but she saw his eyes glance at her in the rearview mirror. They were pale, a light gray, she thought. And they held no hatred, just a frosty coldness. She felt a tiny shiver run down her spine.

She was silent a moment. She could see where they were going. They were almost to a freeway entrance. A traffic light had turned red and they were stopping. Almost instantly a sudden thought translated itself into action. She started to beat against the sides of the truck and scream. If she could attract someone's attention in the cars next to them . . .

The light turned green and they shot away. Marlie waited. The van accelerated onto the freeway. No one followed. No one had heard. One of the curses of a hot, humid city was that most people stayed in air conditioning as much as possible—including their cars, which cut down on outside noise considerably. And if they also had their radios or cassettes playing, little, if any, sound would penetrate.

She dropped her head into her hands. The engine hummed to a steady fifty-five. The man would take no chance with being stopped for speeding.

Marlie thought about her father. Someone would find her car. He would be notified that she didn't get to school, that she was missing. Tears once again sprang into her eyes. He would be so worried.

"Daddy!" she whispered achingly.

Then she was back on her knees at the wire.

"Is it money you want? My father won't give it to you," she lied, knowing that he would give everything he possessed to gain her freedom. "He—he'll tell the police and they'll find you."

The man gave a disdainful laugh.

"Kidnapping is a crime," she tried again. "You don't want to go to jail, do you?"

"I've been in worse places."

What kind of man *was* he? "If you stop the car and let me out now, I won't tell anyone. You can go on your way, no one will come after you."

Her proposition was met with silence.

"I—I have some money...back at the car...in my purse..."

"Just sit still and be quiet." He spoke as if the idea were ridiculous.

"It's not a lot," she continued, grasping at any straw, "but I could get more. I have a bank card...we could go to an automatic teller..."

The man turned his head, momentarily diverting his attention from the road. "Get this straight," he said calmly and yet with an undercurrent of feeling, "I don't want your money and I'm not going to let you go. Nothing you say is going to change what's happened. So you might as well save your breath."

Marlie's light eyes registered the content as well as the spirit of his words. They were wide in her delicately featured face as she watched his attention return to the freeway. In all the books she had ever read, a kidnapper never let the victim see his face—not unless he planned to kill him. Otherwise, the victim could make an identification once he returned to safety.

She swallowed tightly.

"Are—" She had trouble forming the words. "Are you going to kill me?" The pertinent word was wavery.

She saw the man's hands tighten on the wheel. After a long moment, he asked, "If I told you I wasn't, would you believe me?"

"No," Marlie replied huskily.

"Then there's no use in making a reply."

Marlie was still for countless seconds before she dropped to the blanket. Her head lolled back against the metal paneling. For the moment she was unable to continue to fight. She merely let the van propel her forward. To what fate, she didn't know.

Chapter Three

She must have slept. She had no memory of the past few hours, or minutes, or however long she had been unconscious. She worked her arm out from beneath her side and tried to read the face of her watch. In the half-light it was difficult. Two hours had passed.

Marlie pushed into a sitting position. Nothing had changed in the van. The man was still driving, the engine was still steadily eating up the miles, she was still trapped. She raked back the silky hair that had fallen across her face. The van hit a rough spot in the road and she was jolted. She gritted her teeth. Her primary feeling at that moment was apprehension, but along with that emotion was anger. She didn't know what was going to happen to her, but she wasn't going to accept it meekly. Her body had forced her mind to rest; she had been unable to grapple with the swiftly changing events that had occurred that morning. But after her rest, she felt calmer, though not refreshed. Her situation was no longer a surprise to her. She could do nothing about it now, but the man couldn't keep driving forever. They would have to stop—at a destination, for gasoline, to eat…somewhere. And it was then that she would escape.

ONLY IT DIDN'T QUITE WORK OUT that way. To her consternation, she dozed into sleep again. And when they stopped, the first thing she was aware of was the heavy doors opening and the man's strong hands gripping her beneath each arm as she was pulled, struggling, from the van. Her thoughts were woolly, her body not as coordinated as she would have wished, nullifying her plan to get away.

When she was flung over his shoulder, her screech of outrage elicited a gruff "Keep still" while her legs were caught in a steellike grip that prevented any movement. He was strong. She could feel that without really trying. Her weight was nothing to him and her flaying hands, beating against his back, seemed not to affect him. His whipcord muscles moved, adjusting her weight as he began an ascent of a narrow set of stairs.

Marlie stopped fighting long enough to look around. She tried desperately to identify where she might be. There were trees—tall, slender pines mixed with hardwoods—and the house was on stilts. A nearby river must flood on occasion. There was an outhouse—a garage or barn of sorts. Nothing was in especially good repair. The buildings had needed painting for so long that they had attained a weathered look on their exposed wood. And there was nothing else. The house was alone in the wilderness.

She started hitting him once again, twisting, trying to reach his head. If she could knock him out—even for a few seconds—she could run into the woods and hide. But because of the way he held her, she could only reach his back. Suddenly her fingernails curled and she raked them deeply against the material of his shirt. He flinched.

For once she got through to him. She was no longer a fly trying to penetrate an elephant's hide. She had hurt him. The thought satisfied her immensely.

They were at a door that opened onto a short porch. He paused for a moment, unlocking it, then they went inside. He relocked the door immediately, and as she looked around, every window that she could see was barred. He set her on her feet.

Marlie scuttled away, not stopping until she was a distance from him. But her eyes never left him; they were attached to him as if glued. He shifted his shoulders, not from her weight but from her parting blow.

"You're a little hellcat, aren't you?" he grated. His body was tensed for any move that she might make.

"You're only beginning to find out," she retorted. Normally, Marlie was very much a live-and-let-live type of person. But not when she was attacked. Not when someone she loved was attacked. And she felt as if both of those conditions had been met today. Not only was she being hurt, but her father was, as well.

Their eyes raged in silent confrontation. Eventually, he shifted his shoulders again as if the places where she had dug her fingernails into his skin were still smarting.

Marlie took advantage of his momentary diversion of attention and made a quick dash to the door. Maybe it hadn't locked properly, maybe she could force the bar to break. She threw her body against the door, but it was solid, as was the lock. It was shiny and new and definitely meant to keep harm out or a victim in. But Marlie was not in the frame of mind to give up. She continued to throw her body against the wooden door, to rattle the lock.

It took the man to forcibly remove her from her act of desperation. His arms wrapped around her, pulling her away from the door. When she continued to flail around, his arms tightened. She tried to pull away, but he wouldn't let her.

"Stay still! Stop fighting me!" he ordered, his mouth close to her ear. His hands moved, trying to contain her, and his fingers accidentally brushed her breast.

Marlie felt an immediate infusion of heat. And suddenly her mind jumped to another track. He said he hadn't kidnapped her for money...was it rape? Was he some sort of maniac who lured women to out-of-the-way places and violated them?

She began to fight him with renewed vigor. She twisted, she kicked. She tried to hit out at him with anything that could come to hand.

The few seconds were savage. Then, purely through strength, he gained the upper hand and Marlie could no longer strike out. She was panting, her heart drumming a rapid tattoo against her chest, her eyes wild with frenzy. He was breathing hard, as well, his body hot from his struggle.

Through gritted teeth, he rasped, "Have you had enough?"

Marlie glared at him. She hated him—for what he had done to her, for what he was doing. "Go to hell," she spat, her breath coming in gasps.

"I've already been there," he replied.

"I believe it. Let go of me!"

She squirmed against his hold, trying once again to get away. Reflexively, his grip tightened, plastering her to his length.

Suddenly Marlie became very still, aware that she could feel his every muscle, his every sinew, and that every time she moved she only increased the intimacy of their stance.

Just as suddenly, she became aware that he had become still, as well. For the same reason? The thought deeply disturbed her.

Then he was pushing her away, breaking their contact. "You're going to have to stop doing that," he warned.

Marlie's fists clenched at her side as she spun to face him. "What am I supposed to do?" she demanded. "Happily let you rape me?"

"Rape you?" he repeated.

Her chin lifted. "That's what you have in mind, isn't it? Rape me and then get rid of the evidence?"

Some of the tension left his long body. He straightened, taking an easing step to one side. "The thought hadn't occurred to me. Thanks for the suggestion."

"It's not me! It's you!"

"Lady, you have a good imagination."

Marlie's breath came at a gasp. "It is *not* my imagination! Not when— Just now—" She stopped in confusion.

"What are you trying to say?"

Marlie's mouth clamped shut. She was only making things worse. He'd already said the thought hadn't occurred to him. Was she trying to convince him otherwise? She watched him warily, wondering what would happen next.

As she watched, he dug something out of his back pocket. "Here." He thrust an envelope at her. "I was going to wait until you had settled down, but I see that you're not going to settle down until you read this. So shut up and read it."

At first Marlie didn't make any motion to accept it. Then, with trembling fingers she reached out. The face of the envelope was blank, the back sealed.

She hesitated.

"Open it," he directed.

She slid one finger along the flap and carefully withdrew a single sheet of paper. The writing was in her father's hand.

Marlie, forgive me. This is the only way I know to keep you safe. Cord Anderson is the son of an old friend of mine. He'll take care of you, protect you. I know you'll think this is a bit excessive, but under the circumstances, I couldn't take any chances. I had to be sure. I hope it won't have to be for long. Remember my love for you, Dad.

Marlie read the letter a second time, the first reading remaining unclear to her. Her father had played a part in her kidnapping? And if her father was a part of it, could it be termed a kidnapping? In the letter he talked about safety...and protection...and circumstances. What did it all mean? She read the letter a third time, willing it to contain more information than it did. Finally she looked up to find the man's pale eyes resting on her. There was no emotion in his gaze.

"Where did you get this?" she demanded.

"Your father gave it to me."

"I don't believe you."

He shrugged.

"My father wouldn't do this to me!"

"Believe what you like."

Marlie looked at the note again. It was definitely in her father's hand. "Did you make him write this?" She didn't know what was happening, what the reason might be, but she refused to accept this calmly.

The man laughed. The sound wasn't pleasant. It was more mockery than amusement. "Now why would I want to do a thing like that?"

Suspicion was strong in her gaze. "That's what I'm asking you."

Again he shrugged.

Her hand clenched, crushing the note. "I don't believe you. I don't believe this note. It's a forgery. My father would never have anything to do with something this shabby. I don't know what your game is, but I'm not going to play along. Take me home. Now!"

The man's eyes narrowed. "Maybe you don't know your father as well as you think you do."

"I know he'd never hurt me."

"Have you been hurt?"

Marlie thought back to the moments past when she had been held captive against his body. There had been momentary disturbance but she bore no scars, at least not physical ones.

She lifted her chin. "He would never want me to be so badly frightened."

"Maybe it depends upon the circumstances."

"What circumstances?"

"Did you read that note or just skim it?"

"I read it."

"Then...?"

"Then nothing!"

The man took the paper from her unresisting fingers and read it himself. His mouth tightened imperceptibly. "It doesn't say much, but it gets the essence across. What's your problem?"

"My *problem*," she returned heatedly, "is that I don't believe it. I've told you that!" She tapped the crumpled note that he had straightened out. "This says that you're the son of someone my father knows. But I've never heard of you. He's never said anything to me about you."

"I don't expect he has. We don't exactly move in the same circles."

Marlie looked at his hard features, at his look of leashed violence, and she didn't challenge the validity of his statement. He looked as if he'd be more at home in a jungle than in a drawing room.

"And what does he mean by saying you'll protect me? What from? I don't need protecting."

The man's body had remained taut. "Someone's threatened your life. Your father believed him. So you're here."

Marlie stared at him. No. That couldn't be. She shook her head in disbelief. "That doesn't make sense. Who...?" Then she stopped, her memory centering on the man who had been following her.

He interrupted her thoughts, his patience with the subject having drawn to an end. "Does it really make any difference who? It's a fact. Your father's worried and he didn't trust you not to do something stupid—

which, after being around you for the short time that I have, I can completely understand. Hasn't anyone ever told you you're not supposed to aggravate a kidnapper? If I'd been serious about this, you wouldn't be standing here now. You'd be tied up with a rag stuffed down your throat and that pretty face of yours not quite so pretty."

Marlie's claim to bravado took a severe blow at the quiet menace of his words. The lack of doubt in them shook her own conviction. Unquestioningly, if he had been seriously involved in kidnapping her, and not on her father's payroll, her behavior wouldn't have been tolerated. She remembered her fingernails digging into his back, her repeated attempts at escape. She swallowed, trying not to let him know how deeply his harsh statement had affected her. Her tongue came out to moisten her lips. He gave a restive movement that she took to be further impatience.

"I still think I deserve a better explanation than that...than this!" She thumped the note again, striving for calm. "And if I— If I caused any problems, surely you can understand why. What would you do if the same thing happened to you?" Not that she could imagine such a man letting something like that happen; but if it did, his attempts to gain freedom wouldn't have been thwarted. His captor would have rued the day he thought of the plan.

He didn't answer her. He just continued to look at her, during which time Marlie felt decidedly unsure of herself and of her position.

"Are you ready to believe it now?" he asked quietly, still with no emotion.

Marlie ran a distracted hand through her hair. She didn't know what to believe. She hadn't known what to believe since that man had started to follow her and since her father had started to act so strangely. Her thoughts refocused. When the two events were put together . . .

"I'll think about it," she conceded.

He made a sound deep in his throat. It might have meant anything.

She held his gaze even though it was difficult. Finally he murmured that he had to get something from the van and for her not to do anything stupid.

Marlie watched him go, her eyes sweeping his person. He wasn't built particularly powerfully and yet she of all people knew his strength. He was long and rangy and wore his clothes—even the khaki workman's clothes—with easy nonchalance. The muscles were hidden, not obvious.

When she was alone in the room, her first inclination was to bolt from it. To take her chances that he would be waiting for her, ready to implement the plan he had suggested shortly before. But instead she bent to retrieve the letter that had fallen to the floor, her eyes scanning it once again as she straightened. Her body felt detached. So did her mind. She felt as if she had taken a step into the Twilight Zone and had met a pale replica of herself on the other side. Normally at this time of day she would have been leaving the university, her classes completed. She would be arriving home, eating the light lunch that Mrs. Davis, their housekeeper, had prepared; then, since her friend's return, she might have gone over to Regina's to see what she had planned for the rest of the day.

Suddenly she remembered the last time she was at Regina's and her decision to confront the man who had been following her. Her entire body began to tremble as she made her way to a faded chintz-covered chair that mismatched an accompanying couch. She had been going to confront him, demand to know why he was following her and then tell him that he had better stop. Oh, God, what might he have done to her?

Her head shot around when the man reentered the room carrying two of her very own suitcases. Her pupils were dilated with newly discovered fear.

When he met her frightened look, he was irritated. "I'm *not* going to hurt you," he grated.

"It's not that," she whispered, her mouth dry. "I just remembered—"

"What?" He put the suitcases down.

"I think I've seen him."

"Seen who?"

"The man who threatened me. Someone was following me for the last few days. I—"

He didn't let her finish. "Your father hired a guard. It was probably him."

Marlie felt a ridiculous sense of relief. "My father did that?"

Cord Anderson nodded. He nudged a suitcase lightly with the toe of his boot. "This place has only one bedroom. You get it, I'll take the couch."

For some reason, Marlie's heart had jumped. Did she think that he had been going to propose sharing it with her? She felt color come into her cheeks. To cover her reaction, she looked around. What she could see of the house showed that the interior was not in as bad a state of disrepair as the exterior. Someone had

cleaned it recently. There was no dust to be seen; the
floors were freshly mopped. There was no musty,
closed-up smell. There were three doorways leading
off the main room that they occupied. One had to be
the bedroom he spoke of, the other—she hoped—a
bath. The third did not have a door and she could see
that it led to the kitchen.

The man was moving, carrying her cases through
the first door. Marlie rose to follow him. The room
was small in comparison to her bedroom in Houston.
But it was large enough to house a double bed covered with an off-white spread, a chest of drawers that
had seen better days, a nightstand, a lamp and a mirror on which the silver backing had been slowly re-
ceding over numerous years.

"Not exactly Buckingham Palace," the man murmured, watching her reaction.

Marlie didn't let her dismay show. She was not
going to give him an opportunity to ridicule her—
something she sensed he was waiting for.

"It's all right," she said.

The man's pale eyes held steadily on her face, waiting for her to crack. When she didn't, he asked, "Are
you hungry?"

Marlie lifted a shoulder. She wasn't going to admit
to anything that might look like weakness, even if it
had been a long time since her hurried breakfast. Total and complete fear was surprisingly hunger-
inducing—especially when some of the fear was alle-
viated.

"The pantry's stocked," he said. "I don't know if
I got what you like, but it will have to do. We have
enough for a month."

A month? Marlie wanted to protest. But she kept her mouth shut. Now wasn't the time. Instead, she said, "I'm not hard to please."

A glimmer of a smile touched the corner of Cord Anderson's hard mouth. "I'll remember that," he murmured.

Marlie tossed her head, feeling that he had left a lot unsaid. She was trying very hard not to notice how attractive the man was. He was her warder. This was her jail. And even if the cause was a good one, and had her father's blessing, that did not change the circumstance. She had been brought here against her will, under protest, by a man she didn't know, and she would have to stay with him—alone—for a length of time that was indeterminate. It would not do for her to start thinking of him as anything but her captor.

"Would you like me to get the meal?" she asked. The offer seemed to surprise him and she gained an uncommon satisfaction at that feat.

His eyes narrowed but he shook his head. "No, I'll get it this time. We'll take turns."

She nodded silently, holding his gaze.

Something began to tingle along the sensitive webbing of Marlie's nerve endings. Something that began to grow—a hyperawareness that extended from her body to his. Her eyes slid over his features, moving from high cheekbones to patrician nose, to the finely drawn mouth that she found incredibly sensual.

She shook her gaze free with a start, her eyes darkening with shock when she saw that he was examining her in the same way. Then he, too, mentally withdrew, his features resettling into harshness as he turned away.

It was then, for the first time, that Marlie saw the blood. She drew a quick breath and he stopped, partially turning to see what had startled her.

She couldn't get the stain from her mind. The beadings of blood traced exactly her earlier attempt at punishment.

"What is it?" he asked, tensing at her disturbance.

She motioned weakly toward his back. "Did I do that?" she whispered.

"What?" A frown marked his face.

"That . . . on your back."

He moved so that he could see his reflection in the mirror. Not a muscle flinched as he saw the bloodied outline on his shirt. "I guess you did."

"I'm sorry," she whispered huskily.

"I won't die," he said.

Marlie was overcome with guilt. She remembered her feeling of triumph at hurting him. But that had been at another time, when she thought he was her enemy. Not that she didn't think he was any less of an adversary now, but at least she knew he had her well-being at heart—or rather his bank balance. Her stomach lurched. She didn't go around purposely hurting people. She hated the idea of war, of violence. And here she had readily abandoned those high standards, had done so quickly, without giving them a thought.

"I . . ." She swallowed. "I think I'll pass on lunch. I don't feel very well right now."

She felt his gaze bore into her, but she couldn't look at him. She was too ashamed of herself, of her action.

"I've lost more blood than this from a single leech. Don't worry about it."

Her eyes slowly lifted. Was he trying to make her feel better?

"What kind of man *are* you?" she asked, unconsciously repeating the question she had asked herself earlier.

"An ordinary man," he replied.

The answer was short, clipped, giving her the unmistakable impression that he didn't like talking about himself. She veered away from asking herself why.

"I'll get lunch," he said again. "And I think you should try to eat something. You've been through a lot today."

Marlie nodded abstractedly.

He watched her for another moment before finally turning to leave. It was only then that Marlie released the tremulous breath she had been holding.

Chapter Four

William Richards sat with his back to his desk, his face ashen, his eyes focused unseeingly on the panoramic view of the city spread before him.

The deed was done. It had been accomplished even before he left the house to come to the office.

He groaned softly to himself. Marlie was all that he had left. He loved her so. How frightened had she been? He hated that he had been forced to act as he had, but he couldn't see any other course of action. She wouldn't have calmly agreed to leave town for a time. If she had known there was danger, she would have rushed straight into it with the misguided notion that she could look after herself. He knew that she would. It was part of her character. Hadn't she already given him more than adequate proof?

Just two short years before she had been walking along one of the downtown streets and saw a teenager snatch an older woman's purse then take off running toward her. Most people would have stepped aside, but not Marlie. She had seen an opportunity to trip the young thief and had done so. Mercifully, a policeman had been driving nearby, had seen the entire scenario and had hurried to give aid. Then a few years before that, when a neighborhood child was being attacked by a stray dog, had Marlie gone off to find help? No. She had picked up a nearby hose, shot a blast of water to separate the two, and then captured the dog so that it could be confined.

These were not the only incidents. During her entire life, she had made a habit of meeting confrontations head-on, more often than not with a total disregard for her own safety. And if she'd had any idea at all that he, too, had been threatened . . .

William started when his secretary entered the room. He swung around to face her.

"Are you feeling unwell today, Mr. Richards?" the woman asked as she placed a stack of letters on his desk. Her eyes moved over his face, searchingly, with real concern.

William tried to pull himself together; to bring himself from his memories of the past, from the uncertain present and the terrors of the future. He set his expression and cleared his throat. "No, I'm fine. Fine." He straightened the papers for something to do.

She didn't believe him. "Your first appointment is in fifteen minutes. Would you like me to put it off until tomorrow?"

The temptation was great. William wasn't sure if he could make himself concentrate on the case. All he could think of was Marlie and what she was experiencing. Maybe he should have told her. Maybe he could have convinced her.

He cleared his throat again. A fine layer of perspiration had begun to dampen his body and yet he felt cold, so very cold. "No, leave it as it is. I'll be all right.

I just—'' He didn't complete the sentence. He was not aware of not having done so.

The secretary waited, feeling unsure. Something was very wrong and she didn't know what to do. She shifted position. Her movement had no effect on her employer. He just continued to stare at nothing in particular.

''Would you like something to drink?'' she finally asked.

''Coffee? No...'' She had gained some of his attention, but he was still detached.

''I was thinking of something stronger,'' she murmured.

He heard her. His vision visibly cleared. He straightened his back and lifted his head to its usual confident level. ''That's not necessary, Jean. I'm fine. Really. Just let me have a moment or two with these.'' He rattled the letters.

The secretary knew when she was being dismissed. With a professional smile pinned stiffly to her lips, she left the room.

William attempted to read the first letter. It could have been gibberish. He tried again and then let it fall back to the desk top.

Marlie!

MARLIE SAT ACROSS the small wooden kitchen table from her protector. The meal he had prepared was surprisingly good. Not fancy, but good. Or maybe it was just a reaction she was experiencing at having come out of her early-morning nightmare alive and unharmed. When she remembered how frightened she had been...

With a surreptitious glance, she examined the man across from her. Her father knew his father? That was what the note had said. But when? How? She thought she knew all of her father's friends, both business and personal. Before her mother's death, her parents had loved to entertain and she had always been included. There had never been a guest named Anderson. She would have remembered, especially if the father was anything like the son.

Her eyes slipped over him once again. He was a handsome man, but with such an edge of hardness. The deep lines etched on his face, the expression that carefully kept all thought from view, the detached set of his mouth. He looked up and she quickly returned her attention to her nearly empty plate. She felt the intentness of his gaze as she speared a piece of potato with her fork. When he pushed away from the table, his plate and utensils in hand, it was almost a relief.

Water running into the sink signaled what he was doing. Marlie kept her gaze scrupulously away from him. She chewed her bite of food. He came back to sit across from her.

"When you're finished, we need to have a little talk."

Marlie pushed her plate away. "I'm done."

His pale eyes studied her. Then he began, "As I said earlier, there's no way to tell how long this will last. It might be a week, it might be a month, it might be longer. I don't know." Marlie's eyes widened at the last possibility. But when she made no protest, he continued, "So we're going to have to set up some ground rules. First, I'm not being paid to entertain you. There are books, there are magazines—help yourself. Next, as I also said earlier, we're going to share housekeeping responsibilities. I made lunch, I'll make dinner. Starting tomorrow, it's your turn. We'll take it by days. It'll be simpler that way.'' He paused, to give emphasis to his next words. ''Also, in case something happens, I expect you to do as I say. If I tell you to hit the floor, you flatten yourself instantly. If I tell you to get behind me, you get behind me. Is that clear? Because if you hesitate, if you try to question me, you're as good as dead.''

His words hung in the air. Marlie stared at him. No extras, no padding. She cleared her throat and sat slightly forward.

''You speak very calmly of my death. Are you expecting trouble?''

''I believe in being prepared.''

''I still don't understand what's going on. Why it was necessary—''

''It was necessary because that's the way your father wanted it. Nothing more, nothing less.''

''I still don't understand. Why wouldn't he tell me himself? Why would he go to all this trouble? Why would anyone threaten *me*? I haven't done anything to anyone.''

''Another provision is that you don't ask questions.''

Marlie's jaw set in an exact imitation of her father's most stubborn expression. Unconsciously, she did many things that were reminiscent of his way of challenging the world, proximity not heredity being the key.

''I have a right to know.'' Each word was enunciated clearly.

"Your rights ended the moment your father hired me to protect you."

"I don't want your protection. *I* wasn't asked."

"What *you* want doesn't matter."

Marlie's hands tightened into fists on the edge of the table. "How can you say that? At the very least I'm due a complete explanation."

"If your father wanted the situation explained more fully, he would have done it. I've already told you more than he did."

"Only to shut me up!"

Cord Anderson leaned back in his chair and crossed his arms over his chest. "Exactly."

Marlie took a moment to think, then she said coolly and with just the right hint of warning. "It would save both of us a lot of trouble if you'd just tell me all you know."

"Is that a threat?"

"Yes."

He smiled. Dangerously. Yet his voice was soft. "I wouldn't advise you to give me any trouble."

"Because you're bigger than I am and stronger?"

"Because you'd lose."

Marlie was unable to remain seated any longer. Her chair scraped the floor as she jumped up. "It's my life. I deserve to know."

He said nothing, just continued to look at her.

She ground her teeth in frustration. The only door was barred, the windows were barred, the man across from her was as good as barred.

"I want to talk to my father," she said shortly.

"Sorry," was the reply.

"What are you afraid of?" she challenged.

"I'm not afraid of anything."

Now it was her turn to smile thinly, tauntingly. "Oh?"

Cord's lips tightened, all traces of his earlier smile wiped from his face. He pushed away from the table and started toward her.

Marlie began to back away. She was near the door when his longer strides brought him close to her. A strong hand darted out to wrap around her arm. When she felt the fingers tightening like miniature vises, she tried to free herself. The pressure only increased.

"I didn't particularly want this job," he grated. "Baby-sitting a spoiled little rich girl isn't my idea of a good time. But since I committed myself, I'll see it through. It can be easy, or it can be tough—that's up to you. I really don't care."

Marlie had been through so much that day, but she was determined not to let him think that she could be so easily intimidated. She reacted purely on impulse. "If this is too tame for you," she defied, "is it because you're usually on the other side? How much do you charge for a hit, Mr. Anderson?" She looked him up and down. "Why, you're no better than a prostitute. You've already admitted that you're for sale—all we have to do now is settle on your price!"

Immediately she realized she had gone too far. She didn't need the sudden stillness of his body or the tiny gleam of cold anger that sprang to light in his eyes to educate her to that fact. She swallowed, a shaft of fear tightening her throat. But she didn't back down.

"This is a small house," he said icily. "For better or worse, we're going to have to share it. My suggestion is that the less said, the better for both of us."

His fingers fell away. Marlie swayed slightly, rubbing the tender skin. She couldn't break her eyes away from his. She felt like a mouse fascinated by a snake. The danger he exuded was almost hypnotic. He was the first to move, returning to the sink and the dishes that needed attention.

Marlie shivered in the warm room.

THE COZINESS OF the book-lined study did little to succor William Richards that evening. He sat in the chair he had used last night and gazed at the empty one across from him. His heart pounded sickly. He had done the right thing, he had done the only thing. How many times had he told himself that this day? It had been like a litany, to be repeated over and over.

William gave a deep sigh and rubbed his forehead. He felt a thousand years old. And yet with all those years had come little wisdom.

It was easy to fool people, to fool himself. He gave the image of a man who had everything solidly pulled together, who possessed everything he wished—except Monica, and that no man could change. He gave the impression of complete control, of never having made a terrible mistake.

William reached for the bottle he earlier had placed on the table at his side. He tipped some of the contents into a short glass and took a drink. The neat liquid burned his throat, burned his stomach.

A terrible mistake...come back to haunt him. Had the years between meant nothing? On the scale of good and bad, didn't one side outweigh the other?

William took another drink. The fire flared again then lessened.

He had tried to forget. From the first day after realizing what he had done, he had thrust his culpability to the back of his mind. He had gone on, wholly
involved in his life, making his way in the world of
laws and courts—marrying, trying to start a family,
only eventually to adopt. Thinking not at all of the
other man, of the injustice that had been done because of his own guilt.

William's grasp tightened on the glass. If it had been
weaker, it would have broken.

A HAND STILLED its motion in the night, having
reached out yet not quite grasped its quarry. The fly
darted away, landing on the ceiling, safe for the moment from the hunt.

The man stood on the bed, poised for yet another
round. He watched, he waited.

Finally, the fly felt safe enough to move. It swung
low in an arrogance of flight that was rewarded with
capture.

The man laughed as the small creature buzzed
frantically in his hand. That was the way he wanted
Richards to feel—helpless, at his mercy.

The man smashed his hand against the wall. The fly
suddenly ceased its valiant fight for freedom.

MARLIE LAY in the strange bed, unable to sleep. The
reason was not so much the lumpiness of the mattress
as the restlessness of her mind.

After her ill-advised outburst, Cord Anderson had
spoken not a word to her. She knew she wasn't invis-
ible to him. On occasion she had felt his eyes follow
her. But he had said nothing. Not even when he de-

cided it was time to go to bed. She had been sitting on the worn chair, leafing through one of the magazines he must have thought she'd be interested in—she wasn't; the newest fashions and the latest hairstyles didn't matter very much to her—when he merely got up from the couch where he had been sitting and walked across to a closet where he withdrew his bedding for the night. When sheet and blanket were spread satisfactorily on the sagging cushions, he added a pillow and sat down to pull off his boots. Then he stretched out and closed his eyes. That and nothing more.

Marlie adjusted her own sheet and gave a short laugh. She must have stared at him as if he had come from another planet. Also, she was sure that as soon as his head hit the pillow he had fallen instantly asleep. He hadn't snored, it wasn't that. It was his stillness. Not that she could kid herself that he wouldn't be just as instantly awake if she tried to escape.

She lifted herself onto her elbow and thumped a particularly hard spot on her bed. Then she lay down again and stared at the ceiling. The moon was full that night, or near to full. And the curtains were thin. Shadows danced on the walls and on the ceiling as limbs of the nearby trees were blown about by the wind.

What kind of man was he? She had asked that question before. Sometimes he frightened her, but then looking at the harshness of his face could frighten anyone. Yet her father had entrusted her to him. He couldn't be completely bad.

Her father. Marlie's heart skipped a beat. He wouldn't have done this to her unless he was worried almost out of his mind. The danger must have been great. But why? As she had protested earlier, she had done nothing to anyone to cause such a reaction. Her life was dull, actually. She went to her classes at the university, she studied, she went on an occasional outing... nothing to whip up the kind of wrath that would threaten her life.

Her father had been worried, though. He had been acting strangely for the past week. Had he been planning her abduction all along? And just who *was* Cord Anderson? How did he fit into her father's life?

Questions. There seemed to be so many. Were there other secrets that she knew nothing about?

CORD STRETCHED his cramped legs. The couch wasn't nearly long enough for comfort. But he had been in worse places. At least he was dry. He folded his arms beneath his head and closed his eyes again. But this time, sleep didn't come quickly.

She wasn't exactly what he had expected. She hadn't accepted the situation easily. There was a certain amount of nerve. His lips firmed when he thought of her accusation. She had called him a prostitute. And it had hurt. Was that because it came too close to what he gradually realized he had become?

Again the vision of mangled bodies lying in heaps leapt into his mind. Old, young, it hadn't made any difference. And their blood had been on his hands— just as certainly as if he had done the killing himself.

A searing tightness pressed against Cord's chest, making breathing difficult. Bile rose in his throat and his hands bunched into fists until slowly the pressure eased.

Perspiration bathed his body and he could no longer remain still. He rose from the couch to stand at a window. Through the bars he had installed the week before, he looked out into the night. His features were harsh in the wash of moonlight. A gusting wind was tossing the tops of the trees lining the small clearing.

When he was a child, he had loved to sneak out of his room at night and stare at the trees and the sky. Life had been so simple then. There was good, there was evil; there was no blending of the two. He hadn't yet been forced to make hard choices, hadn't seen the degradation man could sink to.

His mouth tightened. Sometimes man was his own worst enemy. The terror of a nuclear warhead was slight in comparison to the terror one person could initiate against others to either gain or retain power. He had been a part of that life, taking the side of whoever paid the most. In the beginning, he had been so innocent—thinking that he could bring some force of good to the world. Fighting against despots who abused their power. Then he had found that despots sometimes had their place and that those who railed against them, when in a position to act, were just as despotic. To the innocents in the way, one was little better than the other. Still he had kept fighting.

A prostitute. She had been more correct than she knew.

Chapter Five

The sound of a fist thumping loudly on her door awakened Marlie from a deep sleep. As she groggily sat up in bed, pushing strands of hair away from her face, the loud thump came again, this time accompanied by a voice.

"It's time to wake up, Miss Richards. You have the honor of making breakfast—and I'm hungry."

"Yes," she managed. "All right."

She heard him move away from the door. It took her another moment to collect herself. At first she hadn't known where she was or who was calling her. Then yesterday had come back with a rush and she had dropped her head into her hands. If it would solve the problem, she would cry. Instead, she struggled out of bed and pulled on a fresh pair of slacks and a blouse from the suitcase she had yet to unpack. She would like to take a shower, but a quick wash would have to do.

She opened the door and peeked into the living room. Gone was his bedding of the night before. The room was also empty of his presence. Before he could return, she hurried to the bathroom and closed herself inside. It was ridiculous to feel this way, but she needed a few more minutes to collect herself. She didn't want to see him yet. She didn't examine the reason; she merely accepted it.

After her quick ablution, she paused to look into the tiny bathroom mirror before exiting the room. She could have used a little makeup, but she hadn't found any. If her father packed her bags, which he probably had, he might have forgotten to add it altogether. Not that she used all that much—a little lipstick, blush, eyebrow pencil and mascara. Her natural blond coloring needed something to make her look less like a ghost. But if the makeup was missing, he would just have to suffer looking at her in her unadulterated state.

She took a deep breath and braced herself for what was to come. When she pulled open the door she saw that he was back in the living room, standing at one of the windows, looking outside. He turned slowly to face her.

Marlie met his steady gaze with pretended calm. He had changed clothes. Today he was wearing worn-looking jeans and a nondescript plaid shirt. His dark hair looked damp. He must have taken a shower earlier, before awakening her, though she had seen no hint of his previous use of the bathroom.

"Good morning," she said, unsure of what to say.

He nodded. His face bore no message.

"You—you said you were hungry. What would you like to eat?"

"What can you fix?"

"What do we have supplies for?"

"The usual."

"Then that's what I'll make. How do you like your eggs?"

"Any way I can get them."

Marlie couldn't help it. She started to smile.

He noticed her reaction. "You think that's funny?" he questioned.

"No, it's just . . . us. We sound so silly."

He made no comment and feeling ridiculous, she moved into the kitchen. Upon inspecting the contents of the pantry, she saw that what he had said was true. There were plenty of basics. Everything she needed, as a matter of fact. She hadn't taken several courses in cooking at the end of her senior year in high school for nothing. At first Regina had teased her, then in the end she had come along, having as much fun learning to create in the kitchen as Marlie had. Some of their experiments had been horrendous, but most had come out fairly well and both girls had enjoyed getting their families together on occasion to plan and carry out dining experiences that never failed to surprise them.

With confidence in her ability, Marlie set about, determined to show him what she could do. Spoiled little rich girl, he had called her. She wasn't spoiled, she wasn't little—not at five foot six—and she wasn't a girl. Twenty-six definitely didn't meet the criterion. Rich—well, maybe a little. But only through luck. She remembered what it was like to do without. The memories were blurry, but they were there. Thirty minutes later she called him.

He stood just inside the doorway, his gaze going first to the table where individual servings of eggs Benedict sat beside a mound of fluffy biscuits and a

plate of cut fresh fruit and then on to her. She poured
their coffee.

"Will this do?" she asked innocently.

Cord Anderson didn't move. Finally he said, "The
supplies have to last. I hope you didn't use them all
up."

She should have expected as much. What was she
trying to prove, anyway? And to him, of all people!

She sat at her place and flicked her paper napkin
onto her lap. Her movements were short, controlled.
"I didn't use too much. There's plenty left."

He moved to take his place, using his napkin more
slowly.

Nothing further was said until the meal was finished. Marlie had totally lost her appetite, but she
wasn't about to let him know that he had gotten to her
again. She chewed each bite as if she were ravenous
and finished with a second cup of coffee.

"That was good," he said at last, with a grudging
show of manners.

"Thank you," she said tightly. She started to gather
the dishes and carry them to the sink. For lunch, he
could expect stale sandwiches.

"No, I mean that," he said. "It was very good."

Marlie paused to look at him. She met his pale gray
gaze. There was very little written on his face or in his
eyes. Still, some of her anger dissipated and she gave
an abbreviated nod. Shortly afterward, he left the
room.

After completing the huge cleanup, Marlie joined
him in the living room. He was reading a well-
thumbed paperback and didn't seem inclined to notice her arrival. She sat for a time, trying to involve

herself in another magazine, then she restlessly got up to move around the small room. She looked out the windows, curiously examining what she could see of the van that had brought them here. He had parked it a short distance from the house in the cover of some tall bushes. Somehow yesterday seemed so far away. A mere twenty-four hours ago she had been driving her car in the sun-drenched warmth of a Houston morning, singing with the music on her car radio, enjoying being alive...and now she was here: in the company of a man she didn't know, for she didn't know how long a period of time.

She sighed and crossed to the chair again. But five minutes later she was up—unable to remain sedentary. Of course, he didn't seem bothered by the inactivity in the least. She wasn't sure if he had moved any muscles except those necessary for life and to turn the book page on occasion.

He must have felt her staring at him because he suddenly looked up. Marlie spun on her heels. She stood at the window, her back to the room, and tapped her toe impatiently.

"You may as well get used to this," came the unwanted advice.

"I'll go crazy if I have to stay here very long," she said without turning around.

"What you need to do is to stop fighting it."

Marlie faced him. "Stop fighting what? I don't know what I'm fighting!"

He marked his place in the book and laid it on the cushion beside him. "Are we back to that again?"

"Yes."

"Why don't you go unpack?" he suggested.

"How do you know I haven't?"

"When I looked in on you this morning, you hadn't. And you haven't had much time since."

He had looked in on her? While she slept? The idea was unsettling. She took refuge in obstinacy. "I don't want to."

"Because you think this will be over soon?"

"If you like."

"I wouldn't count on that, if I were you."

"I can hope."

"Sure, you can do that."

"I will," she said shortly.

When he resumed interest in his book, she paced around the room some more. Fifteen feet by twenty. That was approximately the room's dimensions. And he remained as still as a stone.

After darting him a frustrated look, Marlie went to the bedroom and threw herself on the bed. She *would* go crazy if things continued as they were. She wasn't accustomed to people who kept their distance and their own silence. At least with the people that she knew and loved, when there were silences they were companionable. One person wasn't closing out the other.

She lay on the bed for a long time, dozing on occasion, wakeful on others. She had slept so much over the past day and night. Was it a reaction to the shock she had suffered?

She pushed herself up and her gaze fell on the suitcases. In her hurry this morning, she hadn't worried about wrinkling the contents. And now her clothing was spilling out like so much dirty laundry. If she did as he said and put the clothes away, it would give her something to do. But Marlie rebelled: she *could* hope, she *would* hope. The clothes would stay exactly as they were. What were a few wrinkles between enemies? She wasn't trying to make an impression on him.

But she had done just that with breakfast this morning. Why? Because he had challenged her sense of her own worth? Because he thought that she would be unable to cook; because he thought that she was useless?

Marlie looked at her watch. It was almost time for lunch. And bread took a bit of time to go stale.

CORD WAS ABSORBING very few of the words printed on the pages of the paperback. Without her being aware of it, he had been closely monitoring her every move. William Richards had told him that she was twenty-six, but this morning she looked much younger: scrubbed face, huge blue eyes that both flashed with anger and widened with unconscious innocence.

That innocence made Cord uncomfortable. It had been a long time since he had been near someone so untouched by the uglier aspects of the world. For her, life had always been easy. The pampered daughter of a wealthy, successful lawyer, she had wanted for nothing.

When, eventually, she had stamped into the bedroom, he almost had been relieved. But he knew that the moment she returned, his tension would return with her.

MARLIE DID SERVE sandwiches for lunch. But she couldn't bring herself to sabotage them. After all, there were only so many things one could do with bologna. And she would have to eat it, too.

He made no complaint about the wide variance in their meals. He ate the sandwich just as coolly unemotionally as he had eaten her more elaborately prepared breakfast. Did nothing faze him? Marlie wondered.

She tried to examine him casually. Who was he? *What* was he? A soldier of fortune? A detective? What? He definitely was like no other man she had ever met.

WILLIAM RICHARDS'S HANDS TREMBLED as he clutched the note that had been delivered to his office earlier in the morning. No matter how many times he read it, nothing changed. It was from Doyle Johnson. He knew this, even though it was unsigned.

The man was gloating. He knew that Marlie had been sent away but the fact only seemed to amuse him.

First there was two—now there is one. Do you think you can hide her from me, Richards? I'll find her. And when I do, I'll tell her that she's my child. Do you think she'll believe me? I'll tell her—then I'll kill her. Then I'll come for you. Or maybe I'll come for you first. Isn't it fun to wonder?

The man was insane, completely unbalanced. All the years in prison had unhinged him even more than he had been when William had defended him.

William thought back to that first meeting and cursed the day it had taken place. In his agitation, he crumpled the note into a tight ball.

A MAN, HIS CLOTHING TATTERED and dirty, bumped into another man standing in the shadow of one of the Houston high rises.

"'Scuse me," he murmured, his mind fuzzy from the bottle of wine he recently drank.

"Watch it," came the low, rumbling reply.

The drunk made a series of exaggerated conciliatory hand motions before wandering unsteadily away.

Doyle Johnson returned his gaze to the upper levels of the office building across the street.

Richards had the note by now. Was he enjoying it?

Doyle laughed, a little too long and a little too loudly for normalcy.

And did Richards like the part about telling his daughter that she was *his* child?

Doyle laughed again. That had been a stroke of pure genius. Let him wonder. Let him worry. Let him pay his money and take his chances, wasn't that the saying? You pays your money and you takes your chances.

He liked the way the words rang in his mind. Pays your money...

He shook his head, stopping the words.

Doyle knew all about adoption. Hadn't he been adopted—well, almost adopted? Once he'd almost thought he had a set place to stay until those people decided they liked their cat better than they liked him. And all he'd done was play with it a little. What was a child supposed to do if not play?

Pays your money...takes your chances.

Richards would pay. He would make him pay.

Doyle started to laugh again. He only shut up and moved on when the sun flashed on the badge of one of Houston's finest as he got out of his patrol car.

SEVERAL DAYS PASSED in boring repetition of each other. Marlie had thumbed through every book, every magazine, and her restlessness had merely grown. *He* continued to pretend to be oblivious of her. He would barely talk, giving wonderful laconic imitations of Gary Cooper. Marlie thought she was going to go mad.

Finally she decided to do something about it. After lunch she plopped down on the floor and began some stretching exercises. She felt his eyes settle upon her but she pretended not to notice. If he could ignore her, she could ignore him.

Eventually, when her exercises got to the point where she was running in place, and shaking the entire house in the process—the base perched high on wooden pilings was not conducive to complete stability—he remained silent no longer.

"What exactly are you trying to prove?" he asked.

Marlie continued to run in place. Puffing slightly, she replied, "I'm not trying...to prove...anything. If I can't...exercise...my mind, I'm going...to...exercise...my body."

"Are you planning to do this regularly?"

"There's nothing...else...to do."

"You're going to bring the house down."

"Good. Maybe then...I can go home." She flashed a smile.

He put the book he had been reading aside. His slight smile of return held a certain dryness. "Are you complaining about the accommodations?"

She stopped running. "No," she answered directly, "the host."

He became very still. "I'm not a host. I'm not paid to entertain you. I told you that in the beginning."

Marlie wiped her forehead where tendrils of hair were damply clinging. "Did my father pay you to torture me?" she asked.

His pale eyes studied her. "No," he answered at last. "You know that."

"Then you're doing this for free," she surmised.

"Doing what?" An edge was building in his tone.

"The extra added attraction of solitary confinement."

He frowned. "You don't know what you're talking about."

"But at least *I'm* talking," she challenged.

There was another extended moment of silence. Marlie wanted to twitch under his perusal but she held still.

"Maybe I don't have anything to say," he said at last and reached to collect his book.

She didn't let him off the hook. Before he could bring the book back into place she cried, "I don't believe that!"

The book lowered once again.

"Then let's just say," he explained slowly, "that I don't have anything to say to you."

"Why?" she challenged, her chin rising.

He made no comment.

"Is it because you think I'm stupid? That I'm not your intellectual equal?"

Again he said nothing.

Frustrated, Marlie continued, "I have a bachelor's degree in history. I'm working on my master's. My minor is in sociology. Would you like to debate the state of the world?"

"You're way ahead of me, lady. I didn't go to college."

"Why not?" she shot back immediately. She was determined to keep this conversation going.

He knew her ploy but still answered. "Because I didn't want to."

"Why not? You're intelligent."

"I had other things I wanted to do."

"Like what?"

Suddenly she lost him. A clam was less closed. "Why don't you go take a shower? You look hot."

Marlie debated whether to challenge him again. Whether it would do any good. But she had succeeded somewhat in what she was trying to do. There was always time to try again. A seemingly endless expanse of time. "You're right," she agreed. "I am hot. A shower sounds good."

He made no reply as she stepped in front of him to go to the bedroom to collect her change of clothes. He didn't look up when she moved through the room again on her way to the bath.

The stinging heat of water felt good to Marlie's body. She enjoyed the massage, letting the barrage of droplets move over her head, her neck, her shoulders. In the days before, she had felt awkward about placing herself in so vulnerable a position with Cord

Anderson in the house. Her first shower had been a three-minute affair, with her jumping out almost as quickly as she had jumped in. But she soon learned that she was in no danger. He was not going to disturb her. Somewhere in the back of her mind, she wasn't sure if that fact entirely pleased her. Consciously, it did, but subconsciously...

CORD TRIED TO READ. His eyes scanned the paragraph several times but his mind retained none of it. Much to his disgust, he was all too aware of the water running in the other room, of the fact that just beyond the closed door a woman with a very lithe and attractive body was standing nude.

He remembered the way her limbs had moved as she stretched while she exercised, the way her blouse had parted to give tantalizing glimpses of the curves of her small breasts—she had been totally unaware of what was happening and of his interest—of the way those same breasts had moved while she ran in place.

Cord shifted position. It had been a long time since he had been close to a woman, felt the warmth.

He steadied himself by going to the window to look outside. He leaned against the wooden sill. He had to remember that this was a job. Little different than any other.

The immediate past recurred—the pictures that had been burned in his mind. The bodies of the innocents, twisted, hacked and bullet-ridden. Men, women, children—old and young. Wondatta had given his word. There would be no repercussions. And Cord had believed him. Or had he? Deep in his conscience—if there was any such entity left within him—

did he truly believe that? Or did each drop of blood that had stained the African dust forever remain his responsibility? He should have been there. He could have stopped it. If he had not gone away when directed, the carnage would not have taken place. But he had gone. A pretext. A ruse. Wondatta had wanted him far from the site of his ultimate triumph, of his final victory against an enemy who had already been defeated.

The child—a little girl—no more than two. Her ebony skin still soft and pliant when he picked her up in his arms, a gaping hole where her stomach should have been.

He had fallen to his knees amongst the carnage, tears glittering in his eyes. That was when he knew that he had to get away, that he had seen too much death— done too much, or not done enough.

Cord shook his head, trying to make the memories disappear. Unconsciously he rubbed his palms against the material covering his thighs, as if that action might take away the little girl's blood. And the blood of her family. And of all the others over the years.

A noise behind him caused him to whip around.

MARLIE STOOD IN THE BATHROOM DOORWAY, moist air from her shower billowing into the room before her. Her hair was wet, her white slacks and blue blouse hugging her body, sticky from the humidity.

She stopped short when she saw his face. She had never seen anyone look so . . . so anguished. But intermingled with the anguish was a degree of danger she also had never seen. Instinctively she knew that if she had come upon him unawares in another place, under

other circumstances, her life would be threatened. Her
heart pounded. She was afraid to move. Just in case
her life was threatened by him now.

Cord's long body slowly lost some of its tension.
But enough remained that Marlie's wariness persisted. His handsome features had once again re-
solved into their usual noncommittal state.

"I'm—" She swallowed. "I'm sorry if I startled
you."

He shrugged his shoulders.

She came hesitantly into the room. She didn't know
what to say. He was such an unusual man, such an
enigma. She knew so little about him.

"Ah, you were right. The shower felt great. Maybe
you should try one."

He said nothing. She made an ineffectual movement with her hand.

"I don't think so," he murmured.

She started to turn toward her bedroom to put her
soiled clothing away when he surprised her by saying,
"Would you like to take a walk?"

Her eyes widened with surprise. "You mean...
outside?"

"I don't mean in here."

"Why, yes. Of course. I'd love to."

"Then put your stuff away and come on. I think
we're both going stir crazy."

Marlie didn't take time to enter her room fully; she
just tossed the clothes inside. She was afraid that he
might change his mind.

"I'm ready," she said.

He smiled tightly and motioned for her to come to
the door.

When the lock was released, Marlie felt as a captive bird might when presented once again with freedom. The sun was shining brightly, evading the puffy little white clouds that sailed effortlessly across the sky. A gentle breeze was blowing, enough to play in her hair. A nearby mockingbird was singing its plagiarized song. She took a deep breath and started to step outside, but Cord stopped her.

"Wait," he ordered.

She didn't think to disobey. He pushed his way before her and shielded her body with his own. Once he was satisfied with his survey, he started down the stairs, murmuring for her to follow. He waited for her as he reached the ground, his head swiveling automatically so that his vision could again encompass the area.

"Where would you like to go?" he asked.

"Anywhere," she said with heartfelt sincerity.

They walked side by side along a path. She was aware that he was not relaxed. The tension that had been gripping him earlier had evolved into another type: protecting her was his job; he was intent upon doing it properly. His head moved, his eyes alert to any activity out of the ordinary in the woods. The process seemed to be second nature to him.

"Will you tell me this?" she said, after they had walked a distance in silence, the pungent odors of fallen leaves rising from the forest's sandy floor. "Did my father say who the person is who's threatening me?"

For a moment Marlie thought he might not answer. Then he said, "I didn't ask."

"But did he tell you?" Marlie persisted.

"Why does it matter so much to you?"

"Wouldn't it matter to you?"

He stopped walking. He cocked his head to one side and actually sniffed the air, using his senses like an animal.

"What is it?" she asked. She studied his face but could read nothing from his expression.

"We're near water."

Tension Marlie hadn't known she was experiencing instantly dissipated. She laughed softly. "I've known that ever since we got here. That's why the house is on stilts. I can't believe you weren't aware of it."

He said nothing, but resumed walking. Marlie quickly caught up with him. She slanted him a look. If he had meant his sudden declaration to deflect her from her questioning, he had succeeded. She set her lips. He knew much more than he was telling, she was sure of it. One day, if not now, she was going to get him to talk. But for the moment she let him think that he had distracted her.

Soon, after making their way down a gentle incline, they found the water he had been speaking of. The river was wide and moving sluggishly. Bits of branches floated slowly by, catching occasionally on other branches and debris that lined the bank. Sometimes a branch held, other times it hesitated for only a few seconds before breaking free to continue its journey downstream.

The two of them stood at the river's edge, each thinking his own thoughts. Marlie was aware of him, of the stillness of his long body, of the way he remained alert even as he seemed to relax a degree. A waterfowl of some sort gave a distant cry.

Cord heard the bird's cry and remembered other rivers, many located in not-so-gentle lands—although it wasn't the land's fault that men warred. He started to turn away, to return to the house, but a featherlike touch on his arm stopped him.

"Could we stay here for a while?" she asked, her hand falling away and curling into itself as if it had been burned by the contact.

"I suppose. For a few minutes."

Marlie flashed a smile and quickly found a seat in the shade of a tall, thin maple. Cord looked around once again before finding his own position by a pine.

"I like to watch water," Marlie said eventually. "There's something about the way it moves—" She glanced at him. He was staring across at the other shore where a wall of trees, mostly pines, grew to the waterline. She crossed her legs at the ankles and leaned over to choose a fallen pine needle from a vast array. An ant was hurrying across the sandy soil, intent on an important errand of some kind. She put the pine needle in its path, watching as the insect nearly bumped into it and then quickly scurried around. Lately she had come to feel like such an insect, captured in someone's ant farm—hurrying this way and that, but not knowing why. She sighed. He heard her. She felt the effect of his eyes.

"Are you ready to go back now?" he asked without emotion.

"No." Marlie shook her head. The wind lightly puffed against the maple's leaves, letting a stray beam of sunlight gleam on her pale blond hair. Cord looked away again.

More silence. Finally Marlie asked, "Why did you take this job? You don't know me. My father can't be too close a friend. Oh, I understand that money was involved, but I'm sure a lot of people have more to offer than we do."

"Maybe I needed a change."

Marlie let another second slip by. Then, "From what?"

She looked at him fully, curiously examining the carved cheekbones, the straight nose, the well-disciplined lips. There were lines on his skin that she sensed had more of a history than those caused by exposure to the sun. Exposure to life had given them to him.

"How old are you?" she asked.

He glanced at her. "Why do you want to know?"

She shrugged. "Just curious."

"I'm thirty-eight."

She absorbed the information. "I'm twenty-six," she offered.

"I know."

"What else do you know—about me, I mean?"

"Not much."

She flipped the pine needle she had been holding to the ground. "I know several things about you," she said. His eyebrows lifted slightly. "I know that you've had a hard life and that you don't like to talk very much."

"A regular Sherlock Holmes," he retorted, but with no humor.

She let the comment pass. "Especially not about yourself."

"You see that as a failure?"

"No." She lifted her gaze. "But it does make life difficult. *Your* life, I should expect. You're all tight inside yourself. Like a ball."

"I am what I am," he said shortly. It was easy to see that he was uncomfortable being the subject of investigation.

"I know that, too. You're very secure. Do you never question yourself . . . or what you do?"

He stood up. "We're going back."

Marlie regained her footing more slowly. She brushed the bits and pieces of forest from her jeans. "I'm not being nosy. I'm just making an observation."

He was checking the area around them for any changes. Satisfied that there were none, he turned to her. "I don't like observations."

"Especially when they concern you."

"Correct."

She shrugged then fell into step beside him.

The walk back to the house was made in silence.

Chapter Six

William Richards hung up the telephone after making a series of calls. He now had a name. All he had to do was make an additional call. He lifted the receiver and started to press the digits, then stopped. Did he need more time to rethink his plan of action? To review it one last time to make sure that it could be properly implemented? He let the receiver slide back to its resting place and swiveled his chair until he was in a position to look at the picture of Marlie that now rested on his credenza. It was the most recent photograph that he had of her.

He looked at the sweetness of her expression caught perfectly by the camera, at the gentle intelligence in her eyes. He ran a blunt fingertip along the glass that covered the line of her cheek. She trusted him. She loved him. She believed in him.

What would she think of him if she learned the truth? If she learned that the man who had been so careful to teach her the virtues of honesty, integrity and truth was morally bankrupt? That there was something so terrible in his past, something he was so ashamed of, that he had hidden it for all these years from those around him—even from himself.

William closed his eyes and leaned his head against the back of his chair.

It had all started out so innocently. He had been so young. Trying too hard to make a name for himself. Trying to impress. Ambitious, aggressive, he had wanted to work in the Office of the Public Defender because he thought that would be the quickest way to gain the spot he coveted with the exclusive law firm of Hartman, Hartman and Lowe. He had wanted to dazzle everyone with his ability, and in so doing, had accepted a caseload that was far too crowded. Then he added one more case. One that he didn't think was too difficult.

William slid his reading glasses onto the desk and rubbed his face.

Actually, most of his trouble had come from the fact that the two cases had coincided. The first was his newest case; the second, his golden opportunity. The second had all the makings of an event: it was complicated, sensational and the local media was sure to cover it like a blanket. He would be interviewed repeatedly—he already had. And he knew that with the proper preparation he would win. Hartman, Hartman and Lowe were sure to sit up and take notice. Hadn't the elder Mr. Hartman already complimented him on his handling of the preliminary work?

Doyle Johnson's case had seemed tame in comparison. Simple. Easy. Though he had soon found the error of that line of reasoning. Nothing is as simple as it looks on the surface. No case should be given short shrift in favor of another when it involves a human life.

The case had blown up in his face. What should have been an easy morning in court turned into a nightmare. His ill preparation had showed—even as he tried to bluff his way through—and Doyle Johnson was sentenced to spend most of his life in prison.

Doyle Johnson was an unstable man. From his behavior after the verdict, William knew that he should have used an insanity defense. The man had tried to attack him on the spot—shrieking his innocence, yelling for all the world to hear about William's malpractice.

Somehow he had weathered the storm, winning his next case handily. And pride had mixed with the oil of shame to put his failure behind him. So far behind him, in fact, that he was eventually able to ignore it. Until now.

Marlie couldn't learn of this! William panicked inside. He had always tried to be the best father he could to her. He knew that if he ever saw the light of admiration fade from her eyes he would die. Doyle Johnson would have his revenge without firing a shot.

William sat forward to reach for the telephone. He would not take this lying down. He would not let a madman destroy his life, even if deep down in his conscience he knew that the madman had cause. He would draw Johnson out. Make him tip his hand. Make him forget the care that so far had kept the hands of the police tied.

William cradled the handset to his ear and waited for the ring some distance away to be answered.

MARLIE LAY IN HER BED that night and went over each event of the past few days. She marveled that she had taken everything so calmly. Once having learned the truth, she had behaved relatively well, accepting most of what Cord Anderson said, most of his directives. Why? Ordinarily she would have railed against her enforced imprisonment, even for such a good cause. She would have demanded that she be returned to her father and not kept silent until she had her way. Her protector would have been glad to be rid of her. But she hadn't done that, at least not after the first day.

Was it that she was awed by this man? He was a complete antithesis to everything that she knew. He had been places, done things that she could only guess at. And his silences—they were so filled with taut sparks of electricity. Sometimes she felt it, other times she didn't. But when she did . . .

Marlie had not spent most of her life gaining an education not to be able to reason. She knew that each effect had a cause, each cause an effect. Was her fascination with him a sign of something else? Sometimes she was so aware of him: of the way he moved, of his voice, of his eyes, of the hurt she sensed was hiding beneath the surface of his sternness. Was danger an aphrodisiac? Was she slowly becoming a victim of the Stockholm Syndrome, where captives became enamored of their captors or with their captors' point of view?

But that was silly. Nothing of that sort was going to happen to her. She wouldn't let it. She was only interested in him because he was the lone person she had to talk to. She couldn't exist in an intellectual or an emotional vacuum. She needed conversation, mental stimulation. She tried not to think of any other form of stimulation.

MARLIE AWOKE THE NEXT MORNING to the sound of the shower in the next room. For once, she had awakened before the loud bang of a fist on her door that substituted for an alarm clock.

She swung her feet to the floor. It was her day to cook. She dressed and made her way quietly to the kitchen. She was pouring raw oatmeal into boiling water when she became aware that she was no longer alone in the room.

She glanced over her shoulder. "Good morning," she greeted.

A towel was draped around his neck; his jeans were zipped but the waistband was not snapped. He wore no shirt.

"Good morning."

A tingle of physical awareness shot through her, nullifying her deduction of the night before that he was merely the only person she had to talk to. Something else was definitely involved. The thought unsettled her. She turned back to the stove to continue her preparation of the meal.

"You're up early this morning," he said as he moved into the room. He reached for the coffeepot and filled one of the empty cups sitting on the counter.

"Maybe it's your good influence," she quipped.

He made a disbelieving sound. "At least you make a good cup of coffee." He pretended to toast her after leaning back against the counter.

"A compliment . . . from you?" She darted him a wary glance.

"I'm mellow in the morning."

"I didn't think you were mellow at any time."

"Maybe it's *your* good influence," he returned, choosing to mimic her words.

Marlie shook her head. "I must remember to get up early each morning in the future. I wouldn't want to miss a second of this miracle."

He lapsed into silence, the time for miracles seemingly past.

"The oatmeal will be ready in a few minutes. Would you like a piece of toast?" she asked.

A grunt served as his answer.

That burst of early-morning conversation must have exhausted him because by midday he had barely spoken a total of another ten words to her. Each attempt she made to draw him out was rebuffed.

When she went into the kitchen to make lunch, it was with the determination that the situation was going to change. She would break through his reserve.

Fifteen minutes later she reappeared in the living room carrying a large paper sack.

He looked at her. "What's that?" he asked.

"Our lunch. I thought we'd have a picnic by the river."

Not a muscle moved. "No."

"Why not?" She was not going to be dissuaded. She stood her ground.

"The outing yesterday wasn't meant to become a habit."

"We can't stay cooped up in this house all the time. There's no one out there. Could anyone have followed us here?"

"Probably not," he eventually conceded.

"Then there's no reason not to go outside."

He was silent. The words were there but not spoken.

Marlie gave an exasperated sigh. "I won't try to run away. Good grief, what kind of stupid person do you think I am? If my father thinks I'm in danger—for what reason, I can't imagine—I'll respect his wishes. But if I have to stay inside, with no fresh air and sunshine—with just the whine of that tiny little air conditioner..."

"Why should I believe you?"

"Because you have my word."

Her stand on her honor did little to impress him. In fact, he looked as if he wouldn't trust her if she swore on any number of bibles and crossed her heart a thousand times.

"Don't you believe anyone?" she asked.

He didn't answer. Instead he walked toward the door.

THE DAY WAS A CARBON COPY of the one past: bright sunshine, a gentle breeze, birds calling their joy of life to the world.

"It's beautiful today," she said conversationally as they walked along the path.

"Yes," was his reply. He was acutely aware of everything around them.

They tramped on. Marlie tried again. "I went to camp for a summer once. This reminds me of it. I think I was about ten."

"You slummed?"

Marlie frowned at the innuendo behind his words. "No, definitely not. I was a little girl. I didn't think myself better than anyone else. I still don't. Why do you keep saying things like that?"

He didn't answer.

Marlie stopped walking. "No, I really want to know," she said, causing him to halt as well. He slowly turned to face her. "I realize you don't know me and I don't know you," she continued. "But it *bothers* me when someone thinks I'm something I'm not. You've had this…attitude about me from the beginning. You think I'm spoiled, that I've had an easy life. Well, maybe I have, but should I be punished because of it? And maybe you don't know as much about me as you think you do. Has that thought ever occurred to you? Or do you always go around thinking you're right about everything?"

His pale eyes narrowed under her assault. "Far from it," was his eventual reply.

"Well, that's not the impression you give."

"Impressions aren't everything."

"So we can agree about something," she stated triumphantly. "Not your impressions about me, not mine about you. Doesn't that give us some kind of common ground?"

"We don't need a common ground." He started to walk away.

Marlie hurried to keep up with him, clutching the paper bag. "Common courtesy—that's what I'm talking about. What would it hurt if you were to start a conversation with me once in a while? Do you realize that almost every time you talk to me, it's to give me orders? And when I try to talk to you, you won't."

"I don't talk very much."

"Tell me about it," she said wryly.

She thought she saw a glimmer of a smile touch his lips. It was immediately controlled. They reached the incline and continued to the edge of the river. Sunshine was gleaming on the water, a bird swooped low and then back into the sky.

"How long has it been since you were on a picnic— a real picnic?" Marlie asked as she knelt in the shade of her maple tree and set the bag before her.

Cord made his usual visual sweep of the area then stared across the water.

"Too long," he said and Marlie felt a spurt of success. Yesterday he probably wouldn't have answered that question so readily.

"For me, too," she agreed. "Years and years. And I don't really know why not. I guess it's just something you don't think of doing until you think of doing it." She was rambling, but she didn't want the momentum to stop. "Come sit down," she suggested, glancing at his long, still form. He turned toward her. She patted the ground. "I can't guarantee there won't be ants, but they won't eat much."

She felt his pale eyes remain steadily upon her and forced herself to continue with the preparations for their meal as if she wasn't aware that he was looking at her. Finally he did as she said and settled a short space across from her, folding his long legs like an Indian.

When she had emptied the sack, she asked, "I made roast-beef sandwiches and cheese. Which would you prefer?"

"Roast beef."

She handed one to him then opened a plastic container. "And some fresh veggies." She showed him the carrot and celery strips. "And apples. Will that do? Oh, and a couple of canned soft drinks. You don't drink beer? I couldn't find any in the refrigerator or pantry."

"No," was his one-word reply.

"That's funny," she said before biting into her own sandwich. "I thought you would."

He opened the top on a can of Pepsi. "Impressions, remember?"

Marlie smiled at the reminder. "You're right." She tipped her head to study him. "Just exactly what are you? I mean . . . you're obviously not a policeman."

His laugh was short. "No." He bit into his sandwich.

"Then what?"

"I do a little of this, a little of that."

"For whoever pays the best?" she ventured.

He shrugged.

"Then you're like a mercenary."

Again he said nothing. Marlie decided to change course. He was starting to turn into himself again. "I haven't always had it easy, in case you're interested," she said. "I'm not William Richards' real daughter . . . not his natural daughter. I'm adopted."

"So?"

"So I remember a time when I wasn't. I also remember enough to appreciate what my mother and father did for me."

"Good for you."

Marlie slowly lowered her sandwich. "You sound so bitter sometimes."

He took a long drink and looked out over the water.

Marlie sighed softly. "Would you like a carrot stick?" He took two and crunched on them one at a time until they were eaten.

Marlie finished her sandwich and a carrot stick. She, too, looked out over the water. Would she ever be able to reach him? And exactly why did she want to? Solely because he was so remote?

"I take it you care for your father." His statement surprised her. She was so accustomed to him holding himself aloof.

"Yes, I do. He's very special to me. I'd do anything for him."

"Anything?"

"Yes."

Marlie lost the vision of the river and turned to one inside herself instead—a collage of memories: her father teaching her to tie her shoelaces—a simple thing, but one done with such loving care that she still remembered her tiny fingers struggling and then succeeding and the pride she felt at being able to do as he instructed. She remembered ice-cream cones on hot summer days, a calming hand during afternoon thunderstorms, a gardenia for her hair when she went out on her first date, the pride in his eyes when she received her college diploma...

Then her memories moved on, to the other person who had made her home complete. She murmured, "I loved my mother, too."

"Loved?" He immediately noticed the past tense.

Marlie bit her bottom lip. "My mother died last year...quite suddenly. One day she was fine, the next— My father took it very hard. They had been married for thirty-two years, but he still loved her like the day they married." She paused. "Does that seem silly to you?"

"Why should it?"

"Because...well, because..."

"I'm not an expert. On people or anything else."

"I would have thought you'd have to be...in your line of work."

"No one is an expert in my line of work. Instinct is survival. Experts sit at desks."

"Do, ah, do you enjoy what you do?"

He was silent a long time. "Not always."

"Then why do you do it? Aside from the money, I mean. Does it give you some kind of thrill? Does it make you feel strong, macho?"

He didn't reply but she saw a tightening of his jaw. She decided to retreat once again. "I'll always be grateful to my parents. I often wonder what would have happened if they hadn't opened their world to me. Would I have bounced from foster home to foster home, always wanting a permanent home but never finding it?"

"What about your natural parents? Do you know who they are?"

She shook her head. "When I was younger, I used to make up these wonderful, elaborate stories: my father was a great hero and my mother had to follow him across the globe to wherever he had gone. Then they came back and told me that they wanted me. But my dad heard me playing that way one day and it hurt him so much that I never did it again."

Cord made no further comment and Marlie could think of nothing more to say. She was remembering her father and wondering what he was doing, how he was continuing to react to the worry that had forced him to send her here.

Finally, Cord stood and Marlie followed suit. Wordlessly, they gathered the leftovers and started back on the trail toward the house.

When they were almost home, Marlie said softly, "Thank you, Cord. I appreciate it."

He glanced at her, at her profile, and said nothing.

CORD SPENT THE REST of the afternoon even more quietly than was his custom. He didn't read; he just remained still.

Over the past six to eight years he had come to hold himself separate from the chaos that was taking place around him. That action wasn't a conscious decision, it had just evolved. He operated physically on one level and turned off emotionally on another. He let no one near; friendships were provisional. There was no place for gentleness in his life. Little place for kindness.

Even women had come to be anathema to him. In the areas of the world where he roamed, the type of women who made themselves available were prone to disease and could rarely be trusted. So he had given up even that avenue of comfort. He was a solitary man. And it wasn't until after the turn of recent events that he had come to see how hollow his life had become. There was a vast emptiness inside him, and sometimes it frightened him—he who was frightened of little else.

His gaze automatically flicked to check on his charge's condition, something he did several hundred times a day. She was sitting in the chair opposite him, restlessly trying to become involved in a book. She had been sitting there for some time, something unusual for her. Normally, she seemed to find inactivity difficult and she paced around the room like a caged lioness.

Only this time instead of quickly moving back into his own thoughts, his attention remained upon her, flickering over her person from bright head to small, delicately formed feet. And in his mind echoed the words she had spoken at the end of their outing: she had thanked him, using his name, saying it softly, almost shyly... and she had seemed sincere.

Cord experienced an uncommon feeling of restlessness. One part of his mind told him that he knew exactly what she was doing. He was someone far removed from her usual life and she found him momentarily interesting. She would leave no opportunity untried until she was satisfied that she had cracked his wall of restraint—gotten through to him in some way, for her own amusement. After that, women of her background were quickly bored.

But another part of him contradicted that summation. As she had challenged, he didn't really know her. And what little he did know of her disputed his past assumptions. Instinct, to him, was survival—in any situation, including this one—and there was something he sensed about her that was very different. Honesty...integrity. He didn't believe it, but he sensed it. And there was something else: she was so softly feminine. The graceful way she moved, her quick smile, the gentleness in her eyes when she wasn't challenging him.

He felt his body begin to stir and he immediately halted the process. He didn't need additional problems now. His life was in enough turmoil. He couldn't allow himself to be seduced, by either a gentle look or a touch.

He shifted position on the faded cushion of the couch and forced his thoughts back to other concerns—like what was he going to do with the rest of his life. Continue on the way he had? Or make a change? Only in a recess of his mind that refused to be completely shut away, he remembered how he had responded to the unaccustomed softness of the way she had said his name.

WHEN MARLIE FINISHED cleaning the kitchen after their evening meal, she returned to the living room and sat down with a heavy sigh.

"What I wouldn't give for a newspaper! I never realized how much I'd miss current news. For all we know, invaders from another planet could have landed."

"I seriously doubt that." Cord glanced at her and then away.

Marlie traced the outline of an overblown flower printed on the faded material of her chair's arm. "Well, we wouldn't know, would we?"

"No, I suppose not."

She sighed again. "I don't suppose you have a radio tucked away somewhere."

"Sorry."

"How do you do it?" she demanded. "Don't you get bored with nothing to do?"

"I've trained myself not to get bored."

"I don't think I could ever live that way."

He smiled thinly. "No, I imagine not."

Marlie tilted her head to one side. "You don't think I could do what you do?"

He laughed shortly.

"You don't," she stated.

"Not really."

"I'm tougher than I look."

"I already know that."

Marlie smiled and scooted to the edge of her seat. "Give me a situation. I bet I'll be able to work my way out of it."

"What would you bet?"

Marlie thought for a moment. "If you win, I make our meals again tomorrow. If I win, you do it tomorrow and the next day both. How's that?"

"I'll take it," he said, and Marlie's smile brightened.

"Okay," she said. "Give me something."

He raised a cautioning hand. "Hold on. It has to be something good. I have to think."

Silence pressed between them once again but this time it was more companionable. Marlie was aware of that fact even if he wasn't. She waited patiently.

"Okay," he said at last. "You're coming into an area where you're supposed to meet someone—a friend. All hell is about to bust loose but you're his only way out. The place is quiet. Too quiet. What do you do?''

Marlie stared at him. After a moment she asked, ''Do I have cover? I mean, like bushes or something?''

''Yes.''

''Then I'd wait.''

''For how long?''

Marlie chewed her bottom lip. ''Do I have a way out after I get him?''

''Your own two feet.''

She grinned. ''And I really like him, huh? Enough to risk my life?''

''You're asking too many questions.''

She sobered. ''All right. I'd wait a bit. Then I'd get as close as I could, under cover, of course. Then I'd find a way to see if anyone else was around.'' She looked at him to gauge his reaction. When he merely continued to wait, she went on, ''I'd throw something—a rock—then, if nothing happened, I'd call his name *very* softly.''

''You'd be dead by then.''

''Oh, come on!'' Marlie protested.

''You would. While you were busy throwing your rock, the enemy would have already heard you scuttling through the brush.''

''I didn't know the enemy was so close.''

''You can't take anything for granted—especially your enemy.''

''You didn't tell me he was so close.''

''You have to think for yourself.''

''This wasn't a fair test.''

"In my line of work a person rarely gets a second chance."

Marlie threw him a frustrated look but he didn't relent.

"I'll enjoy the day off tomorrow," he said.

"You don't play fair," she lamented, then shrugged, "but at least it will give me something to do."

"That won't get you killed."

She smiled at him sweetly. "Has anyone ever told you you're a hard man?"

"More than once." A slow smile creased his cheeks. Marlie felt her heartbeat quicken as their gazes locked and then broke away. She cleared her throat. "I wonder what's happening in Houston. What my father's doing. He did call the police, didn't he?"

"I really don't know."

"Is that the truth?"

"Yes."

"But there *are* other things you haven't told me."

"Are you asking a specific question?"

"No, just in general."

"You know all you need to know."

She slid back in her chair. "Do you realize how condescending that sounds? I'm a human being, Cord. I'm an adult. I have feelings. I'm not just some kind of pawn in a game."

"I realize that."

"Do you? Do you really?"

His pale gaze swept over her and Marlie felt herself begin to tremble. A light had been born in his eyes that she was unaccustomed to seeing. Still, she continued her line of reasoning. "Do you realize that you've never said my name? Not once. And we've been here how long—a week? Even under the circumstances, I think you'd call me something. But you seem to go out of your way to avoid it. Is that the way you operate? Completely impersonal? Why, Cord? Are you afraid to get too close to people, to let them see what you are, who you are?''

"That's enough." The light had died in his eyes. They were back to being closed, cold.

"Come on," she taunted, jumping to her feet and smiling at him baitingly. "Say it: Marlie. It won't break your tongue. Try it."

"I think you'd better go to bed."

"I don't *want* to go to bed. I want to stay out here with you. I want to hear you say my name."

"You're acting like a child."

"Now you're trying to say I'm a bad sport because I lost our little bet. It's not that, Cord. I'm just tired of being thought of as a nonentity."

He stood, as well, and for a moment Marlie thought they were going to go through a reenactment of their first encounter in the house. But he remained where he was, not touching her, his hands hanging rigidly at his sides.

"I don't think of you as a nonentity." His voice grated. "No one ever said it was going to be easy to stay in this house with only each other as company."

"Are you telling that to me or to yourself? It wasn't my idea, remember?"

"I should have told your father what he could do with his money. I'm not that desperate. I knew all along I shouldn't have agreed to do this job."

"And don't you think you've made that painfully clear? Why don't you just take me home? Right now.

This minute. I'll explain to my father what's happened and you'll still get paid."

She marched to the door and jarred the locked bar. She rattled it again for good measure.

He was quickly behind her. "Marlie—"

She became very still. She could feel his warmth but not his touch. A vibration of awareness shuddered through her. She swallowed tightly before turning.

"See?" she said softly. "That wasn't so hard." She tilted her head back to look at him.

Cord's first instinct was to strangle her. Then he felt himself become lost in the sweetness of her expression and the blueness of her eyes. For the first time in years, he let himself shift forward, and slowly, carefully, he placed his lips against those of a woman.

Liquid fire coursed through him at the touch, his years of denial bringing back the thirst with devastating force. He pushed her back against the door, melding his body to hers, increasing the pressure on her mouth until his own lips felt bruised. Then, fighting for control, he jerked himself away.

Marlie was breathing heavily, her eyes wide with shock.

"I'm sorry," he said with formal coldness, taking refuge in withdrawal.

Her cheeks were flushed with color. She was watching him as a bird might watch a marauding cat. Cord's mouth firmed even more. He didn't know what had come over him. What had caused him to— Yes, he did. There was no use lying to himself. But he wouldn't let it happen again.

"I'm sorry," he repeated.

"I'm not," Marlie startled him by saying. He tried to mask his confusion as she continued, "At least it proves you're human."

Cord held himself stiffly. "I think you'd better go to bed now, like I suggested earlier."

"I'm not upset, Cord."

He said nothing.

Marlie pushed away from the door. As she crossed the room, she still felt the imprint of the bar, but more vividly she felt the imprint of his hard body. When she said she wasn't upset, she meant angry. She didn't mean a range of other emotions. Her lips tingled even after she changed into her gown and stretched out upon the bed.

CORD SLEPT LITTLE that night, his thoughts unsettled, his body tense. He hoped they would receive word soon that the threat to her life was over.

Chapter Seven

As the days slipped by, William discovered that waiting for such an excruciatingly long period of time was one of the worst agonies a soul can endure. He had set his plan in motion; it didn't hurt to have contacts on the shadier side of legality. But once it was done, he again was forced to wait. He had no idea how long it would take to flush Doyle Johnson out into the open, or even if his attempt would work. Almost daily he received rambling letters that made him cringe when he read them and yet acted as an odd kind of assurance, because as long as Johnson was still making threats against Marlie, that meant he wasn't actively acting against her. At least William clung to that hope. He also wondered what was happening to Marlie, how she was taking her enforced captivity. And Cord Anderson— How much did he really know about the man? He hadn't seen him for what? Twenty years? Just because he was Malcolm Anderson's son, did that mean that he was trustworthy? That William could rely on him not to put Marlie in a worse position than she was already in?

William didn't care so much about his own life. The threats Johnson made against him were bothersome, but he wasn't afraid. It was Marlie he cared about . . . only Marlie.

He reached for another antacid, crunching into the tablet without realizing that his churning stomach had made him reach for like relief only moments before.

DOYLE JOHNSON SCOOPED the tomato soup hungrily, bringing large spoonsful to his mouth. He had almost forgotten to eat today. Sometimes it was like that for him. Time slipped by and he had no memory of it.

He looked at the letter he was attempting to compose as he ate. Richards should enjoy this one, too. He hoped he enjoyed all of them. He took such pains to make them just right—to make them poetic.

A daughter in barter . . . Yes, that was good.

He pushed the finished bowl of soup aside and concentrated on his task. He couldn't let Richards down, not when he was so eagerly awaiting the next dispatch.

MARLIE AWAKENED SLOWLY to morning, as if she were having trouble fighting her way out of her dream. And when at last she did successfully find her way through the mists, she wondered if she truly had achieved reality. Had Cord Anderson kissed her last night? And had she as good as told him that she didn't care? That she didn't mind?

She groaned as she turned over and pulled the pillow over her head. It had happened. She had been awake long into the night thinking about it. In a way, she had forced him to react as he had. She had taunted him, dared him.

She touched her lips under the pillow and remembered the crushing intensity of his. Oh, God!

Marlie also remembered something else. It was her day to cook again. She had lost the bet, and angled toward his winning though it had been, she would keep her bargain.

When she arrived in the kitchen it was to discover Cord standing at the counter, dropping biscuit dough onto a tray with a spoon. He spared her a fleeting glance before resuming his work.

"What are you doing?" she asked as she came to stand behind one of the chairs. "I'm supposed to cook today."

"I decided you were right," he said without turning. "The bet wasn't fair."

"But—"

"I'm taking my turn as usual."

She stopped protesting. She moved to the already perked coffee and poured a cup, taking it to the table where she sat down. The hot liquid warmed her body. When she finished with it, she pushed the empty cup aside and turned speculative eyes upon her companion. He was standing at the stove now, breaking eggs into a skillet. He looked so sternly aloof. Was he trying to pretend that the kiss had never happened?

Never one to leave well enough alone, Marlie cleared her throat and said, "I meant what I said last night, Cord. I'm not at all upset about what happened."

She saw his back stiffen. "Nothing happened."

She gave a soft little laugh, pretending a degree of sophistication that she hadn't earned. "Oh, I wouldn't say that."

He made no reply.

"A bit on the rough side, I should think," she continued, studying her fingernails. "But definitely an interesting kiss."

With studied care he tipped the eggs onto a plate and placed them in the center of the table. Then he took the biscuits from the oven and added them to the fare resting before her. Not once did he look at her.

Driven by a need she didn't completely understand, Marlie couldn't let the matter drop. "Yes, definitely interesting," she added.

"Why don't you keep quiet?"

She feigned innocence. "Am I bothering you?"

He helped himself to one of the eggs and reached for a biscuit. Marlie did the same. She made a slow job of sprinkling pepper, knowing that he was waiting to use the shaker. It was interesting to have him on the defensive, a place she had been for so long during their short acquaintance.

"Whenever you're done, I'd like to use that," he said testily.

"I'm just finishing," she returned sweetly.

When she held the shaker out to him and he reached for it, their fingers touched. The shaker crashed onto the tabletop.

For a moment both of them stared at it. Then Cord pushed away from the table, the chair legs scraping against the linoleum.

"Where are you going?" she called as he walked stiffly away. "Aren't you going to eat?"

"I've lost my appetite," he said shortly.

Marlie's appetite was suddenly gone, as well. She pushed back from the table and followed him into the next room, her exit less hurried.

He was standing at a window, his body taut. She moved toward him cautiously.

"Cord?" she said softly. If anything, his body became even more rigid. "I'm sorry. I didn't mean to upset you. I—"

"I'm not upset. I'm never upset."

"Of course not," she agreed, doubting his words but letting them rest. "I think we're both just getting a little edgy... getting on each other's nerves."

"I'm not paid to have nerves," he returned.

Marlie looked at him in exasperation. "You're human. You proved that last night! So why won't you admit it? You're not some kind of machine that does one job and races on to the next. You have feelings!"

"I'm not paid to have feelings."

"Oh, stop it!" Marlie tugged on his sleeve, trying to make him turn to face her. He remained as he was. "Everyone has feelings, emotions. All right, maybe you didn't enjoy kissing me. Maybe you didn't mean to. But it happened. It's no big deal. My life isn't going to stop because of it and neither is yours."

At that he turned around slowly, his eyes settling on her face. "Kissing comes that easy to you?"

Marlie met his look with steady eyes. "No," she answered honestly.

"You make it sound as if it does."

"And you make it sound as if you have no emotions."

"Maybe I don't."

"I don't believe that."

They continued to look at each other, then Marlie's hand fell away from his arm where it had unconsciously rested. Each took a step back from the other.

Marlie stuffed her hands into the pockets of her slacks. Cord flexed the muscles of his back.

Marlie glanced toward the kitchen. "I'm not really hungry either, but it would be a shame to waste the food."

"You're right," he agreed.

After a moment he motioned for her to precede him into the kitchen. Marlie acquiesced, her steps stilted.

After the meal, Marlie insisted on sharing the duties of cleanup. Cord looked as if he was about to protest but ended up making no dissent.

Marlie wordlessly took her place beside him.

SOME TIME SPENT in the out-of-doors by the river evolved into a daily habit. Cord didn't mean for it to happen, but it did. The house seemed so small sometimes. He hadn't realized how difficult this assignment was going to be for him. He was accustomed to space, to freedom, to being alone. Marlie's company unsettled him. Each day she seemed to eat away bit by bit at the wall he held himself behind. He was growing accustomed to her, accustomed to having her share his space. And with each incursion came more disturbance.

He was attracted to her physically; he would have to be dead not to be. But it was something more. He was attracted to her personality—to the way she thought, to the way she challenged him, to the interest she obviously had in him.

It could be a trap. He knew this. But he seemed powerless to shut himself away completely. Conversation was becoming easier between them. He had told her nothing of himself yet, mainly listening to her as she talked about her life—her father, her friends.

The difficult part of the entire affair was that he was beginning to *want* to talk with her, to share the horror of his last assignment. He had told no one about it; he had told no one about any part of his life. He had no confidant and he had wanted none. Now, strangely, he found himself wanting to tell all to this very young woman, who had tasted so little of life's bitter edge.

Cord relaxed against a slender tree trunk after having given the area another all-encompassing sweep. A bee hummed nearby on its way to either nectar or hive. He closed his eyes for a moment, a part of his soul stirring to the memories of his childhood.

Life in small-town Texas had been simple then, or at least simple to his unknowing gaze. As the only son of a wealthy merchant, he'd had little to care about. He had taken life at face value and not questioned the sometimes resentful glances of the adults around him or the extended silences in his own home. He had lived solely in his own world, engaged in his own pursuits. It was not until later that he saw his father's corruption, his worship of power and the disregard to how it was wielded—or became aware that it was this that eventually had driven his mother away. His father had told him to forget her, that they were better off without her. But, little by little, things had begun to fall into place for him. He knew his mother had taken her only chance and that one day he would take his.

He lost his childhood in the spring of his thirteenth year, along with all respect for his father. And in retaliation for the hurt he felt, he had rebelled. School no longer interested him; he failed more classes than he passed. The embarrassment drove his father wild. To this day, Cord was positive that he had received his high-school diploma only because of the hold his father had over the community.

But before the trouble, there had been days of sweetness, when he was young and carefree, when he had played with his friends in the flowering fields and dreamed all the dreams of youth.

"Cord?" Marlie's voice extracted him from his trancelike state. He sat up instantly, unsure if she was in danger, confused by his momentary inattentiveness.

"What is it?" he asked, his voice tense.

Marlie smiled. "I was just going to ask you a question, that's all."

He resumed his position against the tree trunk, uncomfortable with his memories of his childhood, angry with himself for remembering. "What is it?"

"Do you think we'll be here much longer?"

"I have no idea."

"How are you going to know when it's safe for me to return? How will you find out?"

"I'll know."

She stretched out on the fallen leaves, propping her head against her crooked elbow. "Sometimes this all seems like a dream. Like I'll wake up and be back home in my room."

"It's not a dream."

She sighed. "I know." She was quiet a moment. "I wonder what my professors at the university think—that I've just disappeared?"

"Your father will probably explain."

"That won't help my grades. I guess I'll just have to write off this session and start over again next semester."

"Is there anyone else who will wonder?"

"You mean, about what's happened to me? My neighbor will. In fact, she was worried the last time I saw her. I told her I was being followed."

"I meant a man."

Marlie glanced at him. "There's no man." When he said nothing, she went on. "I've had boyfriends, but no one serious. Dad says I'm particular. But I just haven't met anyone—" She had been going to say "who interested me," but stopped when she realized that she had met someone who interested her and he was sitting just a little ways from her.

She covered her lapse with a yawning stretch. She laughed lightly when she was done.

Cord experienced another pull of attraction. He had the crazy notion to erase the distance between them and draw her into his arms, kiss her—not as he had last night, but sweetly, gently, with infinite care.

She sat up and looked at him with those very blue eyes. He waited for what she would say, her thoughts always surprising him.

"How did you get started doing what you do?" she asked.

The weight of years rushed to press against him. More and more frequently he was beginning to wish that he had chosen another way of life. One where he could feel clean, where he could come to a woman like Marlie without all the shadows of guilt resting on his spirit.

"I answered an ad."

"An ad?"

"An advertisement."

She cocked her head to look at him. "An ad for a mercenary? Are you kidding me?"

"No."

Marlie stared at him disbelievingly. Finally she asked, "What made you do it?"

He shook his head.

"Was it the money?"

"Partly."

"Is it that you like to play soldier?"

"I'm good at it."

She paused. "Have you ever killed anyone?"

"Yes."

"But only when you had to…when you were going to be killed if you didn't?"

He sighed. "It isn't always as easy as that. Sometimes it's hard to tell who's who. Friends and enemies often look alike."

She retreated into silence until questioning quietly, "Does it ever bother you?"

He raked a hand through his hair. How did he explain that sometimes it burned his gut like a live coal? That he had dreams—dreams where all the dead were walking toward him with their wounds hanging open, where a little girl with soft ebony skin and a hole where her stomach should have been was running toward him with a wide smile on her face, as if in welcome.

"Yeah," he said gruffly, "it bothers me."

He could feel the touch of Marlie's gaze on his face, he could feel the tightness of the skin stretching across his cheekbones. He wanted to tell her more, but the words wouldn't come.

She must have sensed that he had said all that he was going to because she looked away, her brow clearing, giving him the opportunity to collect his scattered emotions.

MARLIE GLANCED AT CORD as he stood near her side at the kitchen counter. She looked at his hard features, at the lines experience had drawn on his handsome face, at the loneliness and regret that she sensed were present just under the surface. Then she quickly averted her gaze before he noticed what she was doing. They were preparing the evening meal. Moments before, she had quietly assumed some of the duties and he had done nothing to stop her. They worked in companionable silence until she unconsciously began to hum the melody of a pop tune. Soon soft words fell from her lips in accompaniment. She carved a potato with skill, happily involved in making her own amusement. When she suddenly realized what she was doing, she apologized.

"Why didn't you tell me to shut up? I've been known to frighten small children when I sing."

"I was enjoying it," he said.

Marlie stared at him. "You've got to be kidding."

He glanced at her. "No."

"Then you're a glutton for punishment. I've made voice teachers cry."

"You aren't that bad."

Marlie resumed her work. "I was kicked out of a choir once. I kept hitting all the wrong notes. The director did everything he could to help me. Finally he told my dad that my voice was immature and that I should wait another year or two before trying out again."

"How old were you?"

"Fifteen. He only said that because he was going to retire at the end of that term. If I was mad enough to come back, he wanted to be well away."

Cord laughed and the sound almost made Marlie start because it was so unusual, so rare. He had a nice laugh, she decided.

"Needless to say, I didn't return. I didn't want to go through that humiliation again."

"Maybe the director had a tin ear."

"No. I only wanted to join the choir because my father sang in one when he was young. He has a beautiful voice."

"Which you didn't inherit."

"No..."

Cord heard the regret in her tone and remembered. "That was a stupid thing to say."

Marlie shrugged. "I'm not sensitive about being adopted. I'm really quite lucky."

He looked at her, his eyes running over her face. "Maybe the deal works both ways."

She frowned. "What do you mean?"

"From all the trouble your father's going to, he must feel pretty lucky himself."

Marlie put the last pieces of potato into a pot and filled it with water. "Did he pay you a lot of money?" she asked quietly.

Cord shifted position, curiously uncomfortable at having accepted any fee at all. "A fair amount."

Marlie sighed. "I wish he had told me."

"I don't think he believed you'd come away if he did."

"He was probably right." She thought of the times she had upset her father with what he termed her foolhardiness. He probably felt he had just cause to go to the extreme that he had taken.

She turned to Cord, feeling that this was the correct moment to restate an earlier unanswered question. "How does my father know your father?"

"They grew up together."

"I still don't understand why I've never heard of your family. If they were such good friends—"

"My father doesn't have good friends."

"I don't understand."

"He only uses people. The last time they saw each other, your father came to defend mine in a criminal suit."

"Did he win?"

"My father didn't go to jail, if that's what you're asking. Not that he didn't deserve to rot in a cell."

"You and your father don't get along?" she inquired carefully.

"No."

He put the strips of meat he had been cutting into a marinade. Marlie handed him the pot of potatoes when he reached for it to place on the stove. "That must be horrible for both of you," she said.

"We survive."

"Do you have any brothers or sisters?"

"No."

"Then that's doubly tragic."

"He's not a nice man."

"And you are?" she challenged.

"I never said that. But I don't use people for my own gain."

"What about me?" she asked softly.

The odd light was back in his eyes as he faced her. "I'm giving you a service."

"One I don't want."

"One your father wants."

"And if I say I'm getting tired of being here?"

"Then you'll just have to keep on being tired."

Marlie stared at him. "You really enjoy being tough, don't you? Do you get your jollies pushing old people and children around, too?"

Cord instantly stiffened and Marlie was afraid that her wayward tongue and flash-point temper had destroyed all that she had been trying to build over the past few days. But she would not apologize.

"You don't have the slightest idea what you're talking about," he said stiffly.

"You've said that before."

"That's because it's true."

"Then tell me where I'm wrong. Tell me why you're not some kind of a bully pushing weaker people around. That's what you get paid for, isn't it?"

His hand shot out like a whip to wrap around her arm, jerking her off balance. She came up hard against him. "One day you're going to push me too far," he threatened.

She looked up at him, her eyes wide with alarm. Instantly she became aware of every molecule in her body and almost as equally aware of his. She didn't try to push away or to break his hold.

Cord glared down at her. All too often she hit upon a tender area of his consciousness, reminding him of things he didn't want to think about, much less defend. His fingers tightened momentarily, feeling her tender flesh give. Then he became aware of other things: the way she was pressed tightly against him, the sweet aroma clinging to her hair.

His fingers loosened, only to move slowly up and down her arm. He felt her shudder slightly in reaction, and the heat of madness rushed through him, obliterating all coherent thought. He merely reacted, listening to the urgent whispers of repressed need. His hot eyes wanted to devour her, just as did his body. His arms enfolded her, bringing her even closer, uncaring of her desires if they were different than his. Then, freeing one hand, he positioned her face, keeping her from moving, from pulling away. He bent his head, his lips fixing onto hers.

The heady touch of her soft mouth compounded his intoxication. He moved, pushing forward at the same time as he teased her lips apart. He felt her mouth tremble under his, felt her respond, at first shyly, tentatively, and then with a wave of heat that matched his own. He couldn't get enough of her. His body was on fire and only she could assuage the conflagration.

Marlie was frightened by the depth of her response. When he had pulled her against him and cupped her jaw with his strong fingers, all the breath seemed to leave her body. Then when his mouth had descended on hers like a man driven by a hunger she could only imagine, her body had been swept by such a sweet flame that she barely felt capable of standing. If he hadn't been holding her, she would have fallen. But then, conversely, she had such strength. If he had tried to pull away, to end their pas de deux, she would have fought like a wild thing, not wanting their contact to end, willing it to continue to whatever uncertain destiny might evolve. Her own hands moved on his back, encouraging, enjoying the sensation of discovery. She pressed herself even closer against him, aware of his heat, of his need, of the straining muscles. Her capitulation was complete. Whatever he wanted, he could have. She had never known such a sensation before. It was as if she was dying to herself and becoming a part of him and he of her.

His fingers were at her breast, hurriedly exploring the soft roundness while his mouth blazed a path to the curve of her neck. She felt the first buttons on her blouse give.

Then fear took hold of her once again. This was happening too fast. Much too fast. She was letting her emotions run away with her. She didn't know him. She didn't know anything about him, except the little she'd been able to ferret out. He was so intense: one moment cold and withdrawn; the next, as now, leading her to heights of passion she had never experienced before. He was dangerous. She wasn't ready. They would have to stop.

Marlie fought to regain her balance. The battle was hard. She was dueling with her own emotions as well as his, but at last she managed to break away.

Cord's breathing was erratic as he stared dazedly at her. Her chest was heaving, her body trembling. While he continued to look at her, her cheeks darkened with color and she tried to straighten the disarray of her hair, the wheat-colored threads tangled in a way they hadn't been only moments before.

Slowly he forced himself back to reality. It had happened again: he had lost control. He silently cursed himself with every harsh word that he knew.

Marlie saw the coldness creeping back into his expression and swift tears flooded her eyes. She had been afraid, not just of him, but of herself. But she didn't want him to return to the contained personage she'd had to deal with in the days before. Couldn't he settle somewhere in between? Did he deal only in extremes? She sniffed, automatically taking a step away from his reach. Would he apologize this time?

"I told you you'd push me too far," he said, his voice husky.

She lifted her chin. "So it's my fault?"

He looked at her steadily before admitting quietly, "No, it's not your fault." He turned away from her.

Marlie tried to steady herself. Her voice was as shaky as her limbs. "I'm sorry for what I said. I don't think that about you."

"I don't hurt old people or children."

"I know." His voice sounded so dead. She wished she could think of something more to say.

He spun around to face her. "Do you?" he demanded, taking refuge in anger at her innocent words. "Do you really? Do you *know* what it's like to see people slaughtered like . . . like so many animals, regardless of age and sex? Do you *know* what it's like to hold a child in your arms, a child—" He couldn't go on; his voice broke.

Marlie responded instinctively to his anguish. She moved toward him, but when she reached out to touch his arm, he batted her hand away.

"Cord," she whispered.

The anguish on his face increased.

"Cord, it's all right." She wanted to reassure him. She had never seen such suffering.

"It's *not* all right!" He reacted fiercely.

Suddenly, water from the potatoes boiled over onto the stove. With everything that had happened, Marlie had forgotten that they were cooking. She hurried to remove the pot from the burner. When she turned around, he was no longer in the kitchen.

She stared into the empty space. She knew he wouldn't have gone far, but before she followed him, she had to take a minute to think things through.

She didn't understand what she felt for him, but it was not just a physical reaction to their intimacies of a short time before. It was the man: his strengths, his weaknesses. But how could she approach him—to help him—when he refused to let her near?

Marlie drew a deep breath and squared her shoulders.

She found him standing at one of the front windows. As she moved nearer, his back remained ramrod straight.

Chapter Eight

Marlie approached him slowly. She stopped mere inches away, her stomach fluttering, her body empathizing with his tension.

"Did that happen to you, Cord?" she asked.

Cord heard the compassion in her voice. If she had come to him in salacious curiosity, he could have spurned her interest, rejected her inquisitiveness. But the concern in her voice was his undoing. His hands clenched into fists at his sides as he tried to force the bloody vision from his mind.

"Did it?" she asked again.

The words shattered him. "Yes," he said tightly.

"You killed them?" she whispered.

"As good as."

His body remained taut but hers flooded with relief. He had said that he didn't harm innocent people. But he had also said that the enemy was sometimes hard to differentiate. She had heard many stories of war and the atrocities that were its companion. His life revolved around war of one sort or another. She touched his arm and this time he didn't pull away. "Tell me what happened," she urged.

He was silent for so long that she thought he hadn't heard her. Then, his voice emotionless, he said, "I believed a man. After all the years, after all that I've seen, I believed him. He was educated, he was articulate, he was passionate. He convinced me of his desire to help his people. I should have known—"

In his mind, he saw the camp: the dusty red soil, the blood, the flies swarming over torn flesh. His hands clenched even tighter. Then he worked his fingers, flexing them open and closed.

Marlie remained silent, waiting for him to continue.

"I thought he was different. I thought he really believed what he was saying. But he was just as corrupt as all the others. The moment he took power, the moment we defeated the opposing forces, he began to change. I didn't notice it at first. I was busy with other things. There were still scattered pockets of resistance." He drew a ragged breath. "Little by little, the opposition was contained. When I returned I found that the deposed leader and his staff were being held in the compound—not unusual—but that their families had been detained as well, for their own protection, Wondatta said. Their entire families: mothers, fathers, grandparents, brothers, sisters, wives, children . . . a formidable group.

"Wondatta made a great show of his compassion. He had dinner each day with the man he deposed. He gave gifts to the children." He paused. "His personal physician attended to their needs.

"This went on for weeks. He seemed to be winning them over. Then something came up and I went away for a few days. When I came back . . . When I came back..." His voice broke. He cleared his throat. "When I came back they were all dead. In the holding area. They were slaughtered behind the wire. They didn't stand a chance." Bodies had been left as they dropped—crumpled in heaps, singly. The smell had gagged him.

"But that wasn't your fault," Marlie protested, her eyes dark with the horror he had described.

"I helped put them there. I should have known."

"But how could you know?" she demanded.

"From experience," he replied, his expression stark.

Marlie shook her head. "No. You said yourself he was treating them well, even more than well."

"Maybe that should have tipped me off."

"You're not God. You can't know everything."

"I still should have known...should have realized." Her fingers tightened on his arm. He felt them but couldn't respond. It was as if he were paralyzed to all but one thought. "One of the children—a little girl—she— Whenever I went into the compound she would follow me around. Big dark eyes, a smile that could take your heart away."

"She died, too?" Marlie asked softly. She dreaded his answer but knew that it had to come.

He nodded. He didn't want to tell her. He didn't want to say the words, but he had to. "I found her lying halfway under her mother's body. I recognized her dress. She— Her eyes were still open. But there was nothing there."

His body was as tense as Marlie had ever known it to be. He was sprung like a trap, ready to snap.

"*You* didn't kill her, Cord."

"I did."

"You weren't there."

"Don't you think I haven't tried to tell myself that? But I can't talk it away this time. Not this time. I did it. Just as surely as if I had put a gun to her stomach and tore it away. Her and all the others."

"What did you do after you found them?" Instinctively she knew that she had to lead him forward, to get his mind from the one track it seemed stuck upon.

He shuddered with another quake of memory. He remembered his frenzied search, moving from building to building, tearing down doors, destroying all that got in his way. "I wanted to kill Wondatta. But I couldn't find him. He was very careful to be in hiding. Then his men accompanied me to the airport and put me on a plane. I never saw him again."

Marlie looked at his ravaged face and a fine quiver ran through her body. She wanted to ask more questions, but she knew this wasn't the time. He needed solitude, just as she did, but she couldn't leave him just yet. Not without offering some comfort, even if he didn't want it. "Everyone has something in his past he's not proud of, Cord. Everyone. Some things are big; some are little. But they're there. The hardest job of all is to learn to forgive yourself."

He said nothing. He seemed not to notice when her hand fell away.

She returned to the kitchen. She wasn't hungry. Neither was he, she was sure. But ritual was important in times of distress. She had learned that from her mother during the various small crises that had occurred in their lives. Contrary to what Cord had thought of her upon their earlier acquaintance, her life had not always been easy. No one escapes the process of living without collecting bruises. In her case, grappling with the questions surrounding her past—who her parents were, why they had abandoned her—was her principal concern at times, especially during her teenage years, when so many other questions had cried out for answers. Not that the missing facts of her adoption had ruled her life, but it was there, like a blister that would not heal.

When she finished preparing the meal she called Cord to the table, where he ate mechanically and she barely ate at all.

CORD SAT SLUMPED in the living-room chair, staring at his hands, his mind occupied with both the distant and the near past. Somehow, with the telling, some of his burden had been lifted. Reliving that horrible time, hearing the words spoken aloud, had acted as a catharsis. It was still there, but it was no longer as raw and sore and bleeding. But that he had told her brought its own shame. Was he so weak that he needed another person's absolution? Had he known that she would take his side and tell him that what had occurred wasn't his fault? Had that been in his mind all along?

Cord uttered a muted groan and sat forward to rake his hands through his hair, leaving his head cradled in their support. His life was falling apart. It was self-destructing right before his eyes. And he didn't know what to do about it.

Marlie stepped into the room only to come to an immediate halt. He was sitting in the chair, holding his head, his image that of a man suffering greatly.

Her heart plunged and then wanted to reach out to him. He looked so defeated, a picture she would never have thought to associate with the contained self-assurance he usually projected. He was so strong. So sure. He could handle any situation. Only she knew that he couldn't—at least not one.

When she came farther into the room, he looked up and immediately tried to assume a detached coolness. He started to stand up but changed his mind. If he was wanting to rid himself of her company, there were precious few places for him to go. She settled on the couch opposite him and sent him a fleeting smile.

His expression didn't change. She realized that by now he was probably regretting having told her. But he *had* told her; the words could not be taken back. There was nothing he could do to change that, just as there was nothing he could do to change the past.

She knew that she would have to be the first to speak. If she didn't, the subject would never be raised again. Neither would any other, for that matter. His disclosures would not bode well for conversation in the future.

"I've thought about what you told me," she said levelly. "It was horrible. It must have been horrible to have to live through."

He shrugged, not looking at her.

She plunged on. "But it really wasn't your fault. You *didn't* pull the trigger—"

"At least not this time," he interrupted.

"I didn't think that."

"You could have."

"I'm not dealing with any other time—only this one."

"I didn't tell you to get your compassion."

"I didn't think that you had."

"You caught me at a bad time."

Marlie let that statement pass. If he was going to allude to the moments in the kitchen just before the revelation, she was going to be the one to deflect the conversation. She hadn't let herself think deeply about that yet. And it would be some time before she did. The implications were too confusing. "As I said, you didn't pull the trigger. You didn't kill the child or any of the others there. Your mistake was in believing, in trusting."

"I trust no one."

"You only think you don't. Every time you step on an airplane, you trust. Every time you get in a car."

"You know what I mean."

"Yes, I do. And you know what I mean. You trusted the man. If you hadn't, you wouldn't have left the compound, isn't that correct?"

He nodded, his pale eyes fixed on her face.

"So all you're guilty of is a mistake in judgment."

"A mistake that cost people their lives."

Marlie gave an exasperated sigh. "If you hadn't been there at all, if you had turned the man down when he asked you to work for him, what do you think would have happened? Do you think you made all the difference in the outcome? Would his forces have lost the rebellion without you?"

"No," he admitted quietly. "I'm not that egotistical."

"And the people, would they have lived?"

His answer took a moment. "Probably not."

"I rest my case."

"But I *was* there," he countered. "I saw the people."

"Then all you can do is learn to live with it. You can't change it, no matter how many times you go over it in your mind."

He moved restlessly in his chair. Then he stood up to walk to the window.

"What I have to do," he spoke quietly, looking into the night, "is learn to live with everything."

Marlie gazed at his straight back, at the familiar way he held himself. From their enforced togetherness, she had memorized everything about him, from the way he habitually positioned his head and shoulders to the easy way he walked and stood, his long legs usually encased in jeans.

From the beginning she had sensed a sadness beneath his harsh exterior. She had sensed a loneliness. But never so much as she did now. Unlike Don Quixote, his demons were real. He had no need to set out and search for them. They were there to haunt him, in the day and in the night.

THE LARGE HOUSE in Houston suffered the night with deceptive calm. Uncaring eyes could detect no differences among it and its many neighbors. But three men knew it for what it was: a residence that waited. One, inside, lay in his bed, wakeful and worried, praying that this ordeal would soon be over. Another, outside, blended into the night to keep purposeful watch. And the third, with vengeance on his mind and madness in his soul, stalked the house with inhuman patience.

MARLIE KNEW THE MOMENT she awakened the next morning that the hour was well past her usual time of rising. But there had been no knock on the door, no demand that she start the day. Quickly she jumped from the bed and pulled on her clothing. She stepped quietly through her doorway.

Cord was stretched out on the couch, the bedding tangled, his body restless even as he slept. Marlie instantly came to a stop, surprised that she had caught him unawares. She remained still, watching him. He thrashed around, his features twisted, reliving the past once again.

Marlie stepped forward, conscious of his tortured confession of the night before, her soft heart not wanting to see him continue to suffer. She was almost beside him when he jerked awake. Faster than her eye could follow, he reached under his pillow and was on his feet beside her, the muzzle of a gun pressing against her jaw.

Marlie drew a shocked breath, her body stiff, her heart hammering in her chest.

Cord remained very still, his mind trying to keep pace with his body. When he realized who he was holding captive, he brought the gun down and released his hold.

"Don't sneak up on me like that," he grated in belated warning.

Marlie's hand was at her throat. She gazed at him with stricken eyes. "I wasn't." Her voice was gruff.

Cord stepped away from her and ran a hand through his hair. A night's growth of beard covered his jaw and his eyes were haggard, as if the restless sleep she'd disturbed him from had been all he'd had during the night.

He sank back to the couch and pulled a portion of the covers over his exposed legs. He replaced the gun beneath the pillow.

"I—I didn't realize you had one of those," Marlie whispered.

He raised his head to look at her. "Just what do you think I'm going to protect you with? Words?"

Marlie looked away. "No." Again the word was a whisper.

She heard him sigh deeply. "I'm sorry, okay? But I didn't know it was you."

"You were sleeping," Marlie excused, again strangely wanting to comfort him. She walked to the window and looked outside. The day was overcast, gray and dreary. She heard a noise behind her and glanced over her shoulder to see him pulling on his jeans. She redirected her gaze to the window.

From the sounds behind her, he was folding up his bedding. Once he put it away in the closet, she felt his eyes settle on her. She gave no inkling that she knew he was watching her. Finally, he appeared at her side by the window.

"Beautiful day today," he grunted sarcastically.

"Absolutely," she returned.

His eyes slid over her profile. Cord rubbed his palms against his thighs, uncomfortable with what had happened this morning...with what had happened last night. *All* that had happened last night. He hadn't slept well, remembering.

"I'm sorry I frightened you," he murmured.

She turned to him. "It's all right. I must have frightened you."

His eyes studied her face, trying to see if she was ridiculing him. She wasn't. He moved uneasily again. Every time he looked for some crass motive from her, it wasn't there. She was as she presented herself: an ordinary human being, with no ulterior motives, with no pretensions to be something she was not, with no thoughts of superiority.

His mouth relaxed into a slight smile. "A bit, yes."

She smiled slowly in return. "More than a bit, I should think."

He felt himself becoming drawn to her. He broke away, unable to handle anything more. He moved back to the couch to pull on his boots.

She walked into the kitchen and he heard water being run. Soon he followed her. As they both prepared the meal, little was said. But then little was needed.

While they washed up together afterward, the companionable silence lingered. Marlie began to hum softly, a little off-key admittedly, but Cord didn't wish to stop her. Something was going on inside him, something he would need plenty of time to examine. A spark of something from his distant past seemed to be catching life again. The horrors of Africa still remained; they probably would never disappear completely. But this morning—this moment, at least—they were dulled.

Marlie giggled as she fumbled with a glass while rinsing it—almost losing it, then regaining control at the last possible second. She met his amused gaze and her face seemed to hold all the beauty and promise of life. Cord caught his breath and quickly looked away, using the drying of the glass as his excuse.

THE DAY CLEARED as morning dissolved into afternoon; the sun burned brightly in the sky. Once again, Marlie and Cord followed the path to the river. He still retained vigilant guard, but this trip was different from the others. Marlie no longer felt such a captive. She was here; he was here. But their mutual resentment of that fact was no longer so strongly in evidence.

A cool breeze was blowing off the water as they rested beneath the trees. Wisps of Spanish moss danced lightly in the air as they hung with ghostly presence from the limbs of a nearby oak. A lone cicada cried for rain even though the threat had passed.

Marlie sighed with contentment. She glanced at Cord. He was staring out over the water, his features expressionless. Yet she sensed that he was feeling some of the same contentment as she. She didn't question the emotion; she merely accepted it. She sighed again and drew his attention.

"This is nice, isn't it?" she questioned.

He nodded.

"I suppose you've seen a lot of nice places."

"Some nice, some not so nice."

"What's your favorite place in the world?"

"I don't have a favorite place."

She tilted her head. "Why not?"

He shrugged. A moment passed. "I liked England . . . what I saw of it."

"I've never been there," she replied.

"It's green . . . civilized."

"As opposed to green and *un*civilized?"

He smiled wryly. "Yes."

She tilted her head. "What will you do, Cord? With the rest of your life? I mean, are you going to continue to do what you do now? Or change?"

He was a long time in answering. She waited patiently.

"I've thought about it. I don't know. I don't know what I'm going to do."

"But you don't want to keep—"

She didn't finish the sentence, but he understood. "No, I don't want to keep killing people."

"I didn't say that!" she protested.

"I did." He met her gaze levelly. "I'm tired of it. I'm getting too old for that kind of life."

When he added nothing more, she said, "Thirty-eight isn't old."

"It's too old to keep playing games. And I don't want to ever see—"

He looked away. Marlie studied his classically handsome features. Some of the hardness that had left the line of his jaw as the day progressed had returned. She knew what he was thinking and regretted having brought up the subject.

"You don't have to. There are other jobs."

"For which I'm not wildly qualified."

She thought for a moment. "What about security—executive security? A lot of businessmen are worried about terrorists or kidnappers. Someone with your experience would be a godsend."

He shrugged.

"I'm sure they'd pay well," she said.

He frowned irritably. "Money isn't always the answer to everything."

She blinked. "*You're* saying that?"

His jaw clenched at her barb and Marlie was afraid that she had destroyed the precious calm between them with her last question. It had sounded insulting when, in reality, she hadn't meant it to be.

"I'm sorry," she apologized. "That sounded awful."

He shrugged one shoulder and stood up.

Marlie hurried to her feet as well and went to stand beside him. He noticed her nearness but didn't acknowledge it. She scuffed the toe of her shoe in the sandy earth. A huge ant scurried by. She looked at the treetops swaying slightly in the breeze and asked, "Where are we, Cord?"

"Where do you think?"

"Not far from Houston."

"That's right."

"What river is this?" she asked, motioning to the slow-moving waterway.

"Why do you want to know?"

"Just to know."

"It's one of the forks of the San Jacinto."

"Then we're not far at all!"

"No."

"But we drove so far. Was that to throw off a tail, if we had one?"

He made no reply. She frowned. "I'm worried about my father, how he's holding up."

"I'm sure he's fine."

"Why can't I talk to him? Just a phone call."

"We don't have a phone."

"We could find one."

"No."

"Why not?"

Again he made no reply.

"What are you hiding from me, Cord? What is it? He's all right, isn't he?"

"You saw him after I did."

"I *know* there's something." She searched his face for a clue. It remained impassive. "He started acting weird about a week before I met you. I knew he was worried, but I didn't know what about. I still don't know what about, other than it concerns my life. Cord, who wants to kill me? And why? You owe me that much. Please tell me the truth!"

"If your father had wanted you to know, he would have told you."

"But you know, don't you?"

He said nothing.

She tugged at his sleeve. "Cord, please!"

"If he wanted you to know—"

"Don't say that again!"

"It's the only thing I *can* say."

Her eyes narrowed as an idea occurred to her, one she hadn't thought of before. "I'm sure *I* haven't done anything, so that only leaves him. It has something to do with him, doesn't it?"

"Let's go back to the house. It's getting late."

She wouldn't budge. "It's *his* problem, isn't it, Cord?"

"I'll carry you, if I have to."

She ignored the threat. Her mind was too busy working on the new possibility. "Someone's threatened me because of him. Because of something *he* did. He's in the perfect job for it. He usually wins most of his cases, but if he lost, someone could conceivably think that he threw the case. No matter how good a job is done, some people are never satisfied."

He reached for her and she danced away. "No!" Her eyes were dark with dawning enlightenment. "He wanted me away because we *both* were threatened! That's it, isn't it? He was threatened, too, and he didn't want me to know. That would explain why he didn't want me asking any questions, why you won't tell me anything." She started to bolt away from him but his hand snaked out to stop her. "Let go of me!" she cried.

"Marlie, wait. You can't—"

"I can and I will!" she shouted. She tried to pry his fingers away from her skin. They remained firm.

"Marlie!" His other hand came out to grasp her fully.

She struggled against him, forgetting everything in her concern for her father. It might have been a reenactment of their first day together. "I've got to go to him . . . to help him!"

"You can't do anything," he shouted, trying to get through to her, to make her stop struggling.

Suddenly she stilled and she turned level eyes upon him. "All right, then you go to him."

"I have to stay with you."

"We'll both go."

"No."

Tears of inadequacy spurted into her eyes. She tried to blink them away but was unsuccessful. "I love my father, Cord."

His thumbs moved on her arms. "And he loves you. That's why he did what he did."

"But I can't just—"

"Yes, you can. I'm sure your father has hired his own protection."

Marlie sagged and Cord's grip changed from one of detention to support. "If anything happens to him—"

"It won't."

"How can you be so sure?" She looked up at him, her light eyes reflecting all the emotion she was experiencing.

Cord pulled her into his arms, her head laying against his chest while his chin rested on her hair. "He doesn't want this to drag out," he said quietly. "I'm sure it will all be over soon."

Marlie heard the words. It was as if they had been spoken from far away, then they slowly began to make sense. She lifted her head, causing his chin to fall away. She leaned back to stare at him. "You mean...he's going to do something to make it happen sooner? To make the man come for him?"

"I didn't say that."

"You didn't have to! Oh, God! I know my father. He will! Cord, he will! Are the police helping him?"

"No."

Marlie smothered her cry of anguish. Then a plan began to take shape. She had to get back to Houston, to her father. No matter what it took, she had to get back. She sniffed and made a show of straightening her tumbled hair. She was playing for time while her plan solidified. Cord was not going to let her go, at least not voluntarily.

"I'm sure you're right," she said at last. "I'm just being silly."

Cord frowned, not quiet believing her. She saw his reaction for what it was and hurried to allay his disbelief. "I still wish we'd go back. That way you could protect both of us."

"I'm good, but I'm not that good."

She took advantage of his loosened hold on her arm and slipped from his grasp. She began to walk back along the trail to the house, Cord following her.

Marlie sensed him directly behind her.

They were most of the way back when suddenly she froze. "What's that?" she hissed, pointing into the forest to his right.

Cord immediately jumped in front of her, putting his body between hers and danger. He reached into his shirt for his weapon while searching the area for what she had seen.

Marlie didn't hesitate. This was her chance. Probably the only one she would have. She seized it even if her conscience did pang her at deceiving him, at breaking the promise she had once given. But she had to get back to her father. She had to stop him from taking any kind of chance with his life.

She slipped into a thick stand of brush and then past a windfall of trees and on to another area of brush.

Cord whirled around upon hearing a noise. "Marlie...?" he questioned, but she was gone. She had run away. This had all been a trick! He whipped around again to be sure, but as he suspected, the surrounding forest was silent.

He checked the ground where she had stood, the dirt showing the impressions of her shoes. He saw the direction she took and set off after her, cursing himself for his stupidity. He should have known that she would do something like this.

He followed her trail until the ground changed, making tracking too difficult. He used his other senses, listening intently, narrowing his vision in the contrasting gloom and sunshine. He saw nothing, heard nothing.

Marlie went to ground like a hunted animal. Taking advantage of the limberness of her body, she burrowed to the center of another tree fall, curling into herself, using the entwined limbs and undergrowth for cover. Once inside her hole, she did her best to control the wild beating of her heart and her ragged gasps for breath. She knew that Cord would search for her and she didn't underestimate his abilities. Luck would have to be on her side.

Moments later Cord came silently into her limited range of vision. She squeezed her eyes shut, as if somehow that would help. Her breathing stilled to practically nothing. She waited.

She expected him to call her name. That would have been her instinct. But Cord had other instincts, instincts that had kept him alive under many different circumstances. He silently searched the area, with his gaze, with his keen intellect. She didn't have to see him to know that he was there. Any moment she expected to be discovered.

A noise, coming from another area of the forest, caught his attention. She felt him cease all movement. Then, showing utmost stealth, he followed the direction of the sound.

Marlie's reflexes immediately jumped to life again. Her body tensed, ready to move. If she was to get away, she again had to take advantage of his distraction.

Chapter Nine

Cord suffered great frustration as he stood in a tiny clearing, his hands clenched, his eyes momentarily closed.

He couldn't find her. Even with all his skills, there was nothing he could do. She had disappeared completely, almost as if she had never been there at all.

He ground his teeth and blinked at the brightness of the sun, cursing himself for his stupidity, for his inability to find her.

Then he cursed himself for trusting her.

MARLIE SAT IN A CUSHIONED SEAT, her head leaning against the worn headrest. She was staring at the seat opposite her in the aisle, but she didn't see the person sitting there. She was thinking of Cord, of what he must be doing, of how he must be feeling. By some miracle she had escaped. And she was glad that she had. She needed to be with her father, needed to care for him—to make sure that he would care for himself. But a part of her wished that she had never had to leave. She remembered Cord's face—controlled, in repose, laughing rustily. She remembered their conversations, from the beginning to the very end. Inside herself she cried. Why, she didn't know. She forced her thoughts back to her father.

The bus bounced sluggishly along the highway, covering the distance between the small rural town she had stumbled upon and downtown Houston.

WILLIAM RICHARDS STARED at the brief, willing his concentration not to falter. Hell could be no worse than the punishment he had been forced to endure over the past weeks. Something had to happen soon. He wasn't sure how much more he could abide. He rattled the pages, attempting to read the same sentence a second time.

Voices came from the outer office. Loud voices. William looked up, frowning. His door was thrust open. Automatically he started to stand. The papers fluttered to his desk.

"Dad!" Marlie appeared in the doorway.

William blinked, not believing what he saw.

"Dad...please!"

A man had pushed his way into the office behind her. A scruffy man with none-too-clean clothes. "Is this him?" he demanded.

William's legs felt weak. His mind wasn't prepared to accept what his eyes and his ears were telling him. Marlie was here? Where was Cord Anderson? And who was the individual who was striding toward him? William collapsed back into his chair.

His secretary rushed into the room. "I've called security. They'll be here immediately." She was flustered. In her nine years of working for Hartman,

Hartman, Lowe and Richards, she had never experienced such an occurrence.

"I want my money," the man demanded. "I only bought her bus ticket because she promised me a reward. Now I want it. And I want it in cash . . . green cash. And it better be enough to pay me for my troubles. D'ya hear?"

"Dad, I—" Marlie started to say.

The secretary's head swung around. She stared at the girl. "Miss Richards?" she said blankly. She hadn't recognized her. She looked so different. So . . . She wore absolutely no makeup, her hair was in disarray, her clothes were wrinkled and dirty.

Purely through force of habit William assumed control. He regained his feet even though his legs still felt weak. "If my daughter promised you money, you'll get it. How much?" he asked, turning to Marlie.

"The ticket cost twelve dollars," she said tightly.

William reached for his wallet. "All right. Twelve . . . and a hundred more. Is that satisfactory?"

The man greedily took the money. At that moment two security personnel hurried into the room. The man quickly hid his booty deep in his pocket.

"Mr. Richards?" one officer asked tentatively.

"It's all right. Everything's under control," William heard himself say. "It *is* all right, isn't it, Mr . . . ?"

"Perfectly fine." The man ignored the hint for his name. He started to back toward the door. "Perfectly hunky-dory. She promised me a reward and I made her stick to it."

Everyone looked at Marlie. She held her chin up. "I believe I've already thanked you."

"Yes, you did, little lady. You certainly did. And any time you need another favor—"

"That'll be enough from you," the security guard cut in. "My partner and I will escort you out of the building."

"Fine with me," the man beamed, showing badly stained teeth. He patted his pocket. "Perfectly fine with me."

The security guards hustled him from the room. For a moment William's secretary seemed mesmerized, unable to move. She continued to stare after them.

William cleared his throat to draw her from her trance.

Confusion was in her face and in her eyes as she turned around.

"That will be all, Jean. Thank you," he said quietly.

The secretary's expression made it plain that she still was confused, but she left the room, closing the door behind her.

William felt just as confused, but not for the same reason. He didn't care how Marlie had arrived at his office, just that she was there.

He examined her closely and saw everything that his secretary had. Only he saw something more: worry, fear.

"Did he harm you?" William demanded.

Marlie collapsed into a nearby chair, resting her head for some seconds before answering, "No. I didn't have any money. He caught the bus at the same place I did. That's all."

"I wasn't referring to him." William's eyes bored into her.

Marlie raised her head, her eyes searching his. He looked so stern. New facial lines had been added since she last saw him.

"You mean Cord?" she said.

"Did he harm you? Because if he did—"

"No," she whispered. "No. He didn't hurt me."

"Then what are you doing here?"

Marlie rushed across the space that separated them, rounding the desk, throwing herself into her father's arms. It was wonderful to feel his loving concern, to feel like a child again, protected from all evil. Only she was no longer a child and her father couldn't go on trying to treat her as one. She freed herself, raking wayward strands of hair away from her face.

"I'm here because I ran away."

"He let you go?"

"He didn't *let* me do anything. I ran away."

"Why?" William demanded. "When you were safe."

She tossed her head. "It was because I *was* safe! Dad, I would have appreciated being told."

"I did what I thought was best for you."

"As if I were a child."

"For your protection."

"What about *your* protection?"

William retreated into silence. How did she find out? Had Anderson told her?

"Cord didn't tell me." She anticipated his unasked question. "I worked it out for myself. Dad, what's this all about?"

"I only wanted you to be safe."

"Well, what about me? Don't you think I worry about you?"

"You shouldn't. I can take care of myself."

"And so can I."

"This man is a maniac, Marlie."

She rested her hands on his arm and said softly, "Then that's all the more reason for you to leave town, too. Let the police handle this. Hire someone if you have to. But go somewhere safe. I'll not go anywhere again unless you come with me."

William heard the stubbornness in her words. She wouldn't leave. Not without him. His heart ached. He wasn't worthy of that much love. If she ever found out...

"No. I won't go. I can't run away." He couldn't add cowardice to his list of sins.

"All right, then we stay. But we stay together."

William looked deeply into her eyes.

Another commotion sounded in the outer office. He heard his secretary voicing protest. Then he heard a lower tone—a man's—answer.

The door was again thrust open. Cord Anderson strode into the room, his pale eyes as hard as marbles, his body tense, like a coiled snake ready to strike.

Jean had been trying to bodily keep him from the room and he had pushed her into it before him. She stood there, harassed, on the verge of hysterics. Twice in one day. She glared at the man she remembered from two weeks before. The last time he had come to the office, she had accompanied him. This time, he had barged his way in without bothering to go through security, just as Marlie and that other man had. What good was security if everyone breached it?

"If you don't leave immediately, I'll call the police," she threatened.

"Call the Army if you want. I'm not leaving," Cord replied. He looked at Marlie. "I'm glad you arrived safely."

Marlie was stung by his mocking bitterness.

Once again William had to call up the courage to take charge. "That's enough," he said sharply. Then he visibly reverted to his usual calm demeanor and turned to his secretary. "I think this should be the last of it, Jean. Go back to your office. I can handle the situation now. There's no need to bother security again."

"But—" she protested.

"Everything is fine." William came around the desk to take her arm and accompany her to the doorway. "You know that Mr. Anderson and I have met before, that he came here at my request. So don't worry about anything. Everything is under control."

The secretary didn't look as if she believed him. She darted a quick glance from Cord to Marlie and then back to Cord before William carefully closed the door in her face.

"She's a good secretary," he murmured, turning.

Marlie bit her bottom lip. She felt the tension in Cord. It was like something alive. She was afraid that it would explode.

Her father moved back to his desk. "Well, this has turned out different from what I expected. I thought you were one of the top people in your field, Anderson. You certainly cost enough. Was it too much to ask you to keep her there?"

Cord's jaw tightened even more. He said nothing.

William narrowed his eyes. "Would you like to know how she came to be here?"

"I can speak for myself, Dad."

William ignored her. "Would you, Anderson?" He paused. "She came on a bus. Indebted to the same type of individual I'm paying you to protect her from. Who knows? He might have been in league with Doyle Johnson. Stranger things have happened. And then where would we be? Hmm?"

Some of her father's assumed calm was slipping. Marlie could see it just as easily as she could sense Cord's increasing anger.

Cord walked softly to the desk. His very containment multiplied the danger. "I did protect her," he said shortly.

William didn't back away from the confrontation. "Not from where I stand."

"She ran away."

"Your fault entirely."

Cord clenched his fists. "I can't help it if your daughter is an idiot."

William lunged forward, sending his desk chair scooting against the wall. "You're the idiot around here, Anderson. I paid you to do a job, and you didn't do it."

Marlie tried to step between the two men, but neither would give an inch. "Don't," she cried.

"You let her get away from you," her father continued. "I've half a mind to make you return the money. You certainly aren't going to get the rest of it."

"You can keep it. Every bit of it. I don't want it." Cord reached for his wallet and withdrew a wad of bills that he threw to the desk. "Some of it's gone, but that went on expenses at the safe house. Count it, if you like."

"No. I don't renege on my debts. Take it back and just get out of here. The sooner I *don't* see your face, the happier I'll be."

Cord glanced at Marlie. His features might have been carved of granite. "If you think you're going to have an easier time with her, forget it. She's a stupid little fool."

Marlie received his summation like a knife in the stomach. She sucked in her breath.

If he saw her pain—how could he not?—he gave no indication that he repented his words.

William's face reddened. No one talked about his daughter in that manner. He drew a breath to rush to Marlie's defense when she rushed to her own.

"That's just your wounded ego talking, Cord. How does it feel to be bested?"

His eyes swept over her in contempt. "You think what you did was smart? You could be dead right now."

"Would you care?" she challenged.

His gaze flickered infinitesimally.

"All right, that's enough." William reentered the fray. "Get out of my office. Right now. I don't want to see or hear from you again."

"Gladly," Cord spat and, after gathering the money, left the office without a backward glance.

Marlie's chest felt curiously hollow. He had gone. Just like that. One day he had entered her life in an abrupt manner and now he was leaving it just as abruptly. His name jumped to her lips but it was never uttered.

William raked a trembling hand through his silver hair. When his nerves settled down he would have to think. He would have to make some more calls. Along with his own protection, he would have to ask for more for Marlie. He wondered if he would be able to convince her to stay at home. If he hired several guards, maybe she would be safe. And he would impress on her the importance of not doing anything stupid again.

William kneaded the back of his neck. He had to agree with Cord Anderson there: what she had done had been very stupid. He looked at his daughter. She had sunk into a chair once again and was staring at the door where Anderson had disappeared. She had been through so much. Would she ever forgive him?

He cleared his throat. "Ah, Marlie, you have to understand—"

Her blue eyes raised to him and he was startled by the pain he saw in them.

"Marlie?" he questioned, perplexed.

She shook her head, clearing it. She didn't know what was the matter with her. He was a hateful man—wrapped in his own past, in violence and death. She should be glad to be rid of him and back with her father. But something was missing. Something that knew no name.

"I'm tired, Dad. Do you think we could go home now?"

She sounded a thousand years old. William's heart thumped guiltily. "Of course. Just let me..." He reached for the telephone. Until he had time to garner more protection, he would arrange to have a pair of the building security guards accompany them. He would pull whatever strings were necessary.

Marlie frowned. Seeing the sudden fear that had flashed across her father's face reminded her of why she had come to be in this mess in the first place. Possibly the question should wait, but if she didn't ask it now, would she ever?

"Dad—" The seriousness of her tone stilled his hand. "What did you do to cause all of this?"

Ice crystals formed in William Richards's blood.

CORD PUSHED THROUGH the thick glass door leading from the office building to the street. He was so angry he wished he could have walked straight through it. He needed a physical outlet; he needed some form of action. He didn't see the people who passed by— their startled looks absorbing his anger, or their instinctive recoil. He might have been alone on the sidewalk.

He walked for an unknown period of time, not knowing where he was going, not caring. His anger and his feeling of betrayal carried him on.

Finally, he got a grip on himself and he slipped into a bar. The clink of glasses on small round tabletops blended with low conversation. Businessmen and women were finishing the day, trying to forget their past hours with liquor.

He sidled up to the bar and lifted his weight onto a stool. The bartender took his order for a Scotch and filled it within seconds.

Cord cradled the drink before sipping it. The neat liquor burned its way to his stomach. His emotions had taken a beating that day. He took another sip, turning away from the woman sitting next to him, who gave him an interested look.

Hell, if Marlie wanted to be on her own, let her be on her own. The matter was no longer his responsibility. If her continued protection hadn't been taken from his hands, he would have thrown it back in her father's face on his own. The job had gone sour; it was time to pull away, time to cut his losses and move on. He had the money, most of it. He had done all that he had been paid to do.

He downed the rest of the drink and ordered another.

Apprehension knotted his stomach just as it had when he realized that she had disappeared. At the time, he could scarcely believe that it had happened, that she had escaped. Rage had warred with his own culpability. He should never have let himself trust her. No matter what she said, no matter what she did.

His fingers tightened on the glass. She had asked if he would care if she died. He had run back to the house with that idea paramount in his mind. If she died... If she died... He had wanted to kill her himself. He had wanted to thread his fingers around that delicate little neck of hers... and taste the sweetness of her lips, feel the softness of her body. Her face had haunted him all the while he had canvassed the nearest town and all during the drive back to Houston. Once in the city, he had been unsure where to go first: her home or her father's office. Those were the places he knew she would be drawn toward. He had chosen her home and chosen incorrectly. He hadn't appreciated that further proof of his incompetence.

He was glad to be out of it. He had even turned a nice profit.

His mind stuck on his last thought. That's what his life always boiled down to—making a profit. For years he had done nothing that didn't ensure his own momentary advancement. In the beginning, he had told himself he did it to make sure that he would never again have to be beholden to his father. Slowly, though, his high ideals had evolved into something else, and he had turned a blind eye. Just as he had turned a blind eye to the corruption around him, until the moment he had been forced to confront it and he had become an unwilling witness to the degradation of his soul.

No. This time was different. He had done nothing to be ashamed of. Until he let down his guard. He had told her things he had never told anyone. Things he would never tell anyone again. And she had seemed sympathetic. He had even begun to think that it was possible for a person to change; that mistakes of the past could be forgotten and the future could be lived in some kind of peace; that he could strip himself of what he was and become someone new.

Cord groaned to himself and finished the second drink. He motioned the bartender away when he offered him another refill. He had almost believed.

The curses: greed, callousness and the need for approval. He had fallen prey to each of them. And was one any less destructive than the other?

Cord stared at the neatly arranged row of glasses on the mirrored shelf across from him. He should leave. Everything inside him—every instinct—told him to get on the next plane and leave this state. This country, even. There was nothing more to do here. He wasn't wanted. He wasn't needed. He should turn his back just as he had done many times over the years when faced with the suffering of others. People asked for exactly what they got. No more, no less.

He didn't move.

Chapter Ten

William felt a sickly layer of perspiration break out over his body. Marlie was looking at him, her expression intent. She was waiting for his answer to her question.

What had he done to cause all of this, she had asked. All her life he had done everything he could to make the world perfect for her, as perfect as a father could. He knew there had been problems along the way. He couldn't keep all difficulties at bay. He couldn't take away her early years before she had come into his protective love. He couldn't change the fact of Monica's death—God, how he wished that he could. Monica would tell him what to do now. She would tell him... She would tell him to tell the truth. But he shied away from the truth as if it were a flaming sword that was trying to lure him to his doom.

"I don't know what you mean." He stalled for time.

"But you must," Marlie insisted.

William went over to help her to her feet. "Come on. You've had a rough time. Let's go home, like you said. We can talk about this later."

Marlie resisted. "I think we should talk about it now. I'm tired of being put off, Dad."

William tried to urge her toward the door. "We'll go home, you can have a nice hot bath—"

Marlie jerked away from his grasp. "No!"

William gazed at her, stunned. He had never seen such a look on her face, as if she didn't trust him. His hand slowly fell from her back and he turned away, his backbone stiff, his expression stricken.

Suddenly Marlie wasn't sure if she wanted to know. The look on her father's face before he turned away had frightened her. "What is it, Dad?" she whispered, stepping closer to him.

William whirled around, a surge of anger directed at the man who had caused him to come to such a stage. "Damn Cord Anderson!" he shouted. "Why couldn't he keep his promise?"

Marlie had never seen her father behave like this. Her body began to tremble. No matter what it was, she had to learn the truth that could make him react in this way.

"Leave Cord out of this, Dad. He did everything he could."

"No, he didn't. He let you get away. He put you in danger."

"*He* put me in danger?" she countered with quiet intensity.

William still wanted to shift the blame, to strike out at anyone and anything. He wanted to throw himself from the window—anything to prevent Marlie from finding out. He desperately wanted to keep his position of respect in her eyes, yet he was intelligent enough to see that this time there was no way out. He closed his eyes, only to open them again when he felt Marlie's fingers tentatively come to rest on his arm. Her pretty face was tilted up at him, love and concern in her eyes.

"Please tell me," she pleaded softly.

William drew an unsteady breath as his fingers groped for hers. "It's my fault, Marlie. All my fault." Their fingers wove together and clutched tightly. That action gave him the courage to continue. "A long time ago I defended a man—back when I first started practicing, when I was in the Public Defender's office. I didn't—I didn't mean for it to happen."

When he remained silent for a time, she urged, "For what to happen?"

Eyes that mirrored others she had seen recently looked at her: they were similar in their haunted misery. "I didn't defend him to the best of my ability. I—I thought his trial would be easy. That it was cut and dried. I was concentrating on another trial, one that would make my name." He drew another breath. "I lost it. The man went to jail. He—he just got out, and it seems . . . it seems he still blames me." There was a moment of silence. "And he's right to blame me. Only. . ." He bit his bottom lip as it began to tremble. "He wants to get at me through you."

Marlie wasn't surprised. She already had figured out a great deal of it for herself. "But you're threatened, too," she said.

William nodded, his eyes still cast in misery.

"He must have been in jail for a long time." Her father had been a member of this law firm from the time of her adoption.

"He was sentenced to twenty-eight years. To tell you the truth, I . . . I had forgotten about him. When I received his first letter, I contacted the prison. It seems he's had trouble there, too. He had to serve his full term."

"But if you can prove it's him—"

"I can't! I think he's insane. I think he was then; I should have used that as his defense. But he's smart. There's no way I can prove anything."

"You've talked to the police?"

Her father snorted. "It seems one of us has to be killed before they'll take notice."

Marlie was silent. She didn't know what to say next.

"Now do you understand why I did what I did? Why I had to spirit you away?"

"I would rather that you had told me."

"I couldn't."

"Why not?"

"I couldn't tell you about Johnson. Not without—"

"All attorneys lose a case once in a while."

"Not through negligence."

"Did you appeal?"

Instinctively she had hit upon the real cause of his shame. He hung his head. "No."

Marlie frowned. From being around her father she had picked up a great deal of the process of law. "You didn't?"

"I didn't want to admit that I had made a mistake," William responded. "Johnson was a nobody. He—he was expendable. My career came first."

"Don't say that! That's not the way you think!"

"It's the way I thought then! I bluffed my way out of it, Marlie, and there was no one to care. When they dragged Doyle Johnson off screaming threats, I pretended not to hear. And when anyone asked me about it, I just shrugged. He didn't have any relatives, any friends, any money. And I think he was just crazy enough not to know that he could ask for another lawyer. He—he's stayed in prison all these years, and I forgot about him." He paused. "At least, I wouldn't let myself think about him. I guess he was always there, somewhere in my subconscious. But I just let him rot. While I . . . while I . . ."

Marlie hugged her father. When she felt him begin to shake with remorse, her eyes swam with tears in concert with his. This was so much like what she had heard from Cord. Both men blamed themselves for past mistakes—mistakes that made the present difficult to accept. Both had strong characters and codes of ethics: Cord did, even if he wasn't aware of the fact. That was the reason he was so sickened by the turn his life had taken, by the tragic catalyst of his last job. And her father . . . she knew her father was a good man. He had upheld only the highest principles to her. He had lived those principles.

What he had told her had shaken her. Both for the man who had languished so long in jail, even if he was threatening them, yet mostly for her father, who had divulged such a horrible truth. He had always been like a hero to her, one that lived and breathed and loved her. What did she say to him now? What *could* she say?

Her father took a step back, attempting to regain a measure of control. He rubbed his face to erase the evidence of his tears. "I didn't want you to find out about this, Marlie. I didn't want you ever to know."

She forced a gentle smile. "Why not?"

"I didn't want you to know that I failed you. I don't want to lose you."

Marlie's heart twisted at his poignant cry, its simplicity masking so much grief. Her smile gathered warmth. "How can you think that? You'll never lose me. I love you. From the first moment I ran into your arms, you've been my hero. And you're still my hero now."

Her father shook his head, denying her words.

"Yes," she contradicted. "You have to listen to my definition of what a hero is. A hero isn't someone who doesn't have a flaw, who doesn't make mistakes like the rest of mankind. A hero is someone who accepts his flaws because it's his flaws that make him act as he does, to compensate. Do you understand what I'm saying?"

"Yes, but I think you're being too easy on me."

"You're being hard enough on yourself. You made a mistake, Dad. You're human."

"But my mistake is threatening you."

"I'll survive. I promise. The question now is: will you?"

William Richards gazed into his daughter's blue eyes. If anything, he felt more guilt than he had before. He had abandoned a man in need, one who had trusted him to give the very best of himself, one who'd had so little else to rely on.

All the years, all that he had accomplished, meant little considering that fact. And even if he had worked to make up for the past, striving for a higher plane, never letting an injustice go unnoticed, did that help Doyle Johnson? Did that put things right for him? No. All the people he had assisted didn't make up for that one wrong. Not in Doyle Johnson's eyes, and not in William's. He would have to do something more. Something to help Johnson. To make restitution, if that was possible to do.

Only would he get that chance? Johnson was intent upon killing him and on killing Marlie to get back at him. At the moment, William's first duty was to her.

He drew the most precious jewel of his life into his arms. "I'll survive," he promised her softly. "We'll *both* survive."

WHILE CORD STOOD at the pay telephone, waiting for the ring on the other end to be answered, his eyes skimmed the faces of the people in the bar. So many wore masks, afraid to let the true side of their personalities show. They covered their fear with laughter and small talk, pretending to be someone they weren't.

The completed connection drew his attention. A gruff voice said a name.

"R.J.? This is Cord." He spoke quickly, concisely. "I'm calling back that debt you owe me. How soon can you be in Houston?"

There was a moment's silence on the other end of the line. Then, "Will tonight be too late?"

"No. But make it as early as you can. I need your help."

"I figured that," came the dry reply.

Cord smiled tightly. He pictured the man as he had last seen him: sitting smack in the middle of a bevy of beautiful Salvadoran women, lifting a bottle of te-

quila in the air and telling anyone who would listen—
at the top of his lungs—that he was through with that
"shitty little business." That he was going to go back
to Louisiana and he was going to open a dry-cleaning
establishment and the closest he wanted to come to a
bomb again was the one he would use to kill roaches.

"I can be there by ten," the man said.

"Come to this address." Cord gave him William
Richards's home address. "I'll meet you a little way
down the street."

"Right. See you later."

Cord hung up without replying.

WHEN MARLIE ENTERED her home, months seemed to
have passed since the last time she had claimed its
shelter. In fact, it was not quite two weeks. But so
much had happened in that time. She felt immeasur-
ably older.

Her father couldn't seem to do enough for her. It
was as if he were trying to make up for everything that
had happened, everything that might happen.

"Would you like something to eat? I'll call Mrs.
Davis and see if she'll whip something up for you before she leaves. Why don't you sit down? You look
tired."

Marlie *was* tired. She didn't realize just how tired
until now. But she had to stop her father's solicita-
tions. Normally he was a considerate man, but at the
moment, he was carrying concern too far. She didn't
think that it was good for him.

"I'm fine, Dad. Really."

He pulled her toward a chair anyway. "Just sit here. I'll at least put some coffee on. Now, don't tell me that you'd refuse coffee."

Marlie found a smile. It was no use. He was determined. "That sounds great."

"Good. I'll be right back."

Her smile faded as her father hurriedly left the room. Two of the building security guards had accompanied them home and her father assured her that his own guard was in place as well and that he would soon be joined by another duo of private guards. But even with the numbers, she didn't feel as safe as she had with Cord.

Cord. Where was he now? What was he doing? Her father had struck out so angrily against him and he had reacted in kind. She remembered his eyes, the way he had looked at her. Resentment, fury, bitterness, betrayal. He had looked as if he hated her.

Marlie went to stand at one of the long windows, her fingers clutching the heavy drapery material as she pulled it aside. She stared into the deepening twilight. When she heard her father's return, she started to turn but was startled by his sharp shout. "Marlie! Don't do that!"

The horror in his voice paralyzed her. She didn't know what was happening.

William put the tray he had been carrying on a table and rushed to rearrange the curtain in place. "Never stand in a lighted window—that was the first thing I was told. You make too good a target."

She smiled thinly. "I find it hard to think of our home as a prison."

"I know. I do, too."

Marlie moved to the tray to pour the coffee. She prepared her father's just as she did her own, with cream and nothing else. "Do you think this will go on much longer?" she asked as she handed him his cup.

"God, I hope not," William murmured fervently.

"What do you think will happen to...Johnson? Was that his name?"

William nodded as he sipped his coffee. His eyes followed Marlie as she resumed her place in the chair. "I don't know, honey. I think that's going to depend on him."

She sighed. The faint marks under her eyes were more pronounced than usual. Her body seemed to droop with weariness. But William sensed that she wanted to talk and if listening to her was something he could do for her, he would do it.

"You really believe he'll do this?" she asked.

"I can't take a chance and not believe it."

"You were very hard on Cord. He did take excellent care of me."

William stifled his irritation. "I'm sure he did."

"He would have given his life for mine," she murmured. Her words were beginning to slur. She had not taken her own cup. It remained on the tray.

"That's what he was paid to do."

"No... No, I mean...he would. He would actually do it even if he hadn't been paid."

A spurt of another kind of fear shot through William. What was she saying? What had passed between the two of them at that safe house? But before he could question her further, William saw that she had fallen asleep.

Her head was tipped to one side and her blond hair was spread over the dark material of the cushion. She looked like a child again: soft and trusting and so very vulnerable.

William's heart compressed with love. She was his little girl; his baby. The one he and Monica had waited so long to have. She had enriched their lives every day that she had been with them. He would do whatever he must to protect her... against anything, or anyone.

His steps were muted as he came to lift her into his arms. A smile flickered on her lips as her head came to rest against his chest. William saw the smile and wondered at its cause.

CORD MOVED THROUGH the sticky night air. A mosquito landed on his arm. Unconsciously, he slapped it away. He had been at the Richards residence for three hours now and it had taken him less than three minutes of that time to spot each of the guards. He kept out of their way, not drawing the men's attention. It was a measure of both his ability and the guards' incompetence that he had been able to do so.

He checked his watch. It was almost ten. He moved carefully toward the street, angling away from the house, using the shrubbery as cover. The lots in this area were large. There was a lot of room to negotiate. He moved toward the intersecting street, blending with shadows, keeping low to the ground.

At exactly ten o'clock a car approached. When it started to turn onto the street, Cord stepped into the light. The car immediately pulled to the edge of the road and Cord went to meet his compatriot.

R.J. Thibodeaux was not a large man. Neither was
he young, being somewhere in his middle fifties. His
hair was cut short and was graying from its once pure
black state. His features were like those of a genial
puppy: alert, curious, always ready to play. He would
have been a great grandfather, if he had taken the time
to have children. But there was another side to R.J.
Thibodeaux, one Cord had seen intimately: R.J. never
ran from danger, and he was an artist with an Uzi.
Until the day he decided that he'd had enough. Then
he had dropped from sight to live on his bayou in
Louisiana, cleaning other people's shirts with utter
contentment.

Cord slipped into the passenger seat and pulled the
door shut. He felt R.J.'s quick appraisal. "I appreciate you coming," he murmured.

R.J. clapped him on the back. "For the man who
saved my life not once but twice, anything."

Cord smiled slightly in return.

"What's up?" R.J. asked.

"I want to set up a surveillance. Two people. A man
and his daughter. Someone wants to kill them."

"And the father's hired you. Why call me?"

"I can't do it alone."

"That old bugaboo sleep gets you every time. Keeps
us from thinking that we're superhuman."

"Something like that," Cord conceded. "Also
they'll probably separate."

"Why do I get the feeling there's something you're
not telling me?"

Cord was silent a moment. "Officially I'm not on
the job. I was fired."

"Then why stay?" He paused. "Oh! Now I get it. How old did you say the daughter is?"

Cord frowned. So far he had not let himself ponder his reasons. He was merely listening to a voice that made him stay, that made him call R.J.—that frustrated him severely.

"I'm surprised at you, my friend," R.J. was saying. "I thought you were beyond such things."

His amicable teasing made Cord twitch in his seat. "It's not that," he denied.

R.J. beamed with pleasure. "I think it's exactly that. You've been caught, my friend. Like a rat in a trap. Otherwise you wouldn't be doing this."

Cord's frown increased. The dim light from a street lamp filtered into the window to show his intensity. He shook his head and his friend laughed.

Cord swung his door open. "Go back to your bayou, R.J. Sorry I bothered you." He was preparing to step onto the sidewalk when a hand shot out to stop him. The fingers were like steel talons on his arm.

"No. I apologize. What you do and why you do it are not my business. If you need help, I help."

Cord's pale eyes met the almost black eyes of his friend. Long seconds passed. Then Cord eased himself back into the seat. R.J. released his grip and flexed his fingers before resting his arm once again on the steering wheel.

"Now," R.J. asked, "what would you like me to do?"

CORD TOOK THE FIRST WATCH. After hearing the details of the plan, R.J. had gone off to find himself a place to put his things. He would return a couple of hours after midnight to spell Cord so that in the morning they both would be ready for whatever might come. If the two Richardses separated, R.J. would watch William and Cord would watch Marlie. At night they would take turns.

Cord positioned himself where he could see the house to best advantage and where he could not be seen. His mouth curled in disdain when he saw the gleam of a cigarette that one of the hired guards was smoking. Why didn't the man set off fireworks to mark his position?

Cord shifted, moving away from the stubble of a branch that was poking into his back. He would stay in this position for a time and then move on, keeping a complete watch, not letting too much time go by before moving somewhere else. The front of the house was lit from the street and from its own subtle outdoor lighting. It was the sides and the back that worried him. That was where his attention would be more concentrated. As he watched, a light was switched on in an upstairs room. He wondered if the room belonged to Marlie.

Chapter Eleven

Marlie awoke the next morning and stretched in the softness of her bed, vaguely aware that something was wrong. Her eyes opened. She was in Houston! Back in the spaciousness of her bedroom that was decorated with her favorite colors. Gone was the tiny house built on stilts close to a river in the East Texas woods. Gone was the decaying mirror, the mismatched furniture, the lumpy bed. No longer would a fist pound on her door announcing the arrival of a new day. No longer would she have to share in the preparation of meals. At one time she would have given everything she possessed to be here, where she was safe and loved. Now all she felt was a great hollowness.

She had to forget him. He didn't care for her, just as she didn't care for him. There had been nothing between them . . . No, that was a lie. There *had* been something between them. Something that—

A knock sounded on her door and caused her to start violently. Her father's head soon showed around the door's edge. When he saw the vestiges of her reaction, he looked momentarily ashamed, but that didn't keep him from continuing into the room. He was carrying a tray.

"I didn't think," he explained. "Your nerves have a right to be all keyed up. I thought—I thought you might enjoy breakfast up here."

Marlie tried to find a smile. She sat up, positioning pillows behind her back and straightening the silk coverlet. Her father arranged the tray in front of her before carefully sitting on the edge of the bed. The tray contained coffee, orange juice, a piece of toast and cereal.

William observed his daughter as she pushed stray strands of hair away from her face. "You look rested," he said.

"I am."

He sighed deeply. "I slept a little better myself last night. Probably because you're home. I worried about you when you were away."

Marlie reached for the small glass of orange juice, her fingers trembling slightly. The orange juice tasted good to her. She hadn't had any for the past ten days.

William hung his head, his eyes seeing only his loosely clasped hands. Last night, before going to sleep, he had wrestled with his options for the days ahead. He could stay home, with Marlie, or he could go about his life as he always had—going into the office and into court—to try to draw Johnson to himself. He decided on the latter. She would be as safe here as he could make her. One guard would come with him—he knew she wouldn't allow anything else—one would remain in the house and another outside. Johnson was smart. He wouldn't strike where he was outnumbered.

"I've decided to go to work today." He heard the beginnings of her protest but continued, "I've a case I can't assign to anyone else. I have to go, Marlie."

Marlie moved the tray from her lap; she couldn't eat. She sat forward. "I don't think you should do that. If we stay together, it will be easier for the guards to protect us. If we separate—"

"We've been separated until now. I didn't stay home all that time. I went about my business and I fully intend to continue doing that."

"But that was before—" I knew you were in danger, too, she had been going to say when her father interrupted.

"Marlie, I have to do this, for my self-respect. I'll have protection, I promise."

Marlie didn't want to agree. The reason she had come back was to force him to take care of himself. But what he had told her yesterday had changed that. She could see that he needed to face his past in order to face his future. She leaned close to hug him.

"You'll be careful?" she asked tightly.

"I'll be careful." He pulled away slightly to gaze at her. "And you? You'll do exactly as the guards tell you? You won't do anything foolish?"

Marlie bit her bottom lip and shook her head in agreement. "The most I'll do is go over to Regina's."

"Have Regina come over here."

"What did you tell her while I was away? What reason did you give?"

"I said you'd been called away."

"And she didn't question that?"

Her father laughed gruffly. "Of course she questioned it. I just put her off, that's all."

Marlie's expression lightened. "I can see I'll have my hands full trying to explain."

"That should keep you busy," William agreed. He pushed to his feet. "Eat that breakfast. Mrs. Davis will worry if you don't."

"What did you tell *her*?" Marlie asked dryly.

"The same thing."

She groaned. Her explanations would have to be made in duplicate.

William paused at the door. "I'll see you later this afternoon."

Marlie gazed at him and nodded tightly.

When she was once again alone, she settled back against the pillows and adjusted the coverlet over her legs. She even drew the tray into position. But it was a long time before she began to eat.

REGINA STARED AT HER, unable to believe what she was hearing. "He had you kidnapped?" she repeated, amazed.

Marlie smiled at her friend's shocked expression. "Abducted is more accurate."

"But why?"

Marlie glanced at the guard who had followed them into the garden. He was big and burly and not too intelligent-looking, a complete opposite to Cord. He was standing near the wide French doors that led into the sitting room. She moved away from him, letting her fingers trail along the delicately scented petals of a row of rose bushes in full bloom. Regina moved to her side.

"Do you remember the last time I saw you, when I told you that I was being followed?"

Regina nodded. "Yes. Oh, no! It was true?"

"I'm afraid it was. Someone had threatened my life. The man was a guard my father hired to watch over me."

"Oh, Marlie!"

"My father's been threatened, too. That's why—" She motioned toward the man who had remained by the house. Regina followed the direction of her hand. "We each have someone watching us," Marlie continued.

"But who? Why?" Regina's face was pale, her eyes large. Marlie might have been telling her that she had sprouted wings and could now fly. But she believed her; she always had.

"Someone my father once defended. He...he's got a grudge. He just got out of jail and..."

Regina suddenly searched the area around them as if terrorists were ready to descend. "Let's go inside. We shouldn't be out here."

"No. It's all right. I've lived with this for two weeks, Regina. I can't...I can't stay locked up all the time. The guard is here and there's another one around somewhere. My father's gone to his office and then into court. We can't let this man rule us entirely."

"But your father was so afraid that he had you abducted."

"He went a bit overboard."

"He told me that you had been called away."

Marlie smiled slightly. "Did you believe him?"

"Not really. He looked so funny...so tense. Where were you taken?"

"Not too far, actually. Just outside the city."

"Were you afraid?"

"At first."

"Who took you? Him?" Regina indicated the man who was now leaning against the house, one leg drawn up at the knee so that his foot could rest against the brick. He wasn't looking at them. He was studying his fingernails. A feather of unease again disturbed Marlie's security when she remembered Cord's vigilance.

"No."

She felt Regina's gaze return to her face. She didn't meet her curious look.

"Who, then?" Regina asked.

Marlie squeezed her hands together, rubbing one palm with the opposite thumb, an action she sometimes surrendered to when disturbed. "A man."

Regina's eyes narrowed. There had been unspoken emotion in her friend's reply. That, coupled with her obvious discomfort, further peaked Regina's curiosity. "Where's the man now?"

"My father fired him."

Regina blinked in surprise. "This is beginning to sound like a plot for a movie."

Marlie laughed hollowly. "A bad one, right?"

"Not necessarily." Regina drew a breath. "Why did your father fire him?"

"Because I escaped and came back to Houston on my own."

"He wasn't a very good guard, then."

"Don't say that. He was. He—" Marlie bit her bottom lip to prevent herself from continuing.

If Regina had entertained suspicions before, they were underscored now. "How did you get away?"

"I got him to trust me. But I didn't do that with the idea of getting away. I just . . . when I found out that my father was in danger, I just . . . took advantage of his trust.''

"What was he like?'' Regina asked slowly.

Marlie shrugged.

Regina darted another look at the guard who was still acting as if he didn't know that they were there. "Did he look like him?''

"Not at all.''

"Somehow I didn't think so,'' Regina murmured dryly.

Marlie's cheeks darkened. She dipped her head to smell a flower in order to hide her face from her friend. But she was afraid that the action had been wasted.

"What did you do all that time while you were with him?''

Marlie lifted her head. "Not very much. There was no radio, no television. I cooked.''

Regina smiled. "You mean he used *you* as a servant?''

"We took turns by days.''

"Sounds exciting.''

"And we talked.''

"That sounds exciting, too.''

"It was. He . . . he's had an interesting life.''

"What is he? A private detective?''

"No.'' Marlie started to walk back toward the house. Regina fell into step beside her.

"What's his name?'' Regina asked when Marlie said no more.

"What difference does it make?''

"I'd just like to know.''

"His name is Cord Anderson.''

At that, Regina discovered what she wanted to know. When Marlie said his name, there was a wealth of conflicting emotions in her voice, but most prominent was longing. Her friend had fallen in love. It might not be the kind to last, considering the circumstances, but it was very real. And she wasn't sure that Marlie was completely aware of it. She treated her friend with tenderness, hooking her arm through hers as they approached the French doors.

"Well, my life hasn't exactly been standing still while you were away. The situation with my mother is getting worse and I can't seem to do anything about it. I've tried. One day last week I was all ready to get everything off my chest, but I couldn't do it. I just know she's going to take it the wrong way and be hurt. And I don't want to hurt her—I just want her to treat me like an adult. I don't know how much more of this I can stand."

Marlie tried to listen attentively while Regina complained. She knew that she wasn't the only person in the world experiencing difficulties, but she wasn't sure how to help her friend. She knew that Regina and her mother loved each other and she suspected that the difficulties they were now experiencing were the result of leftover scars from the growing-up process. Her only thought was that if they would just try harder to understand each other. Understanding why people do what they do means so much. That was why she felt so close to her father during his present crisis and why she had felt so close to Cord. Cord. Thinking his name both hurt and thrilled her. What was the matter with her? Why couldn't she forget him?

THE HOTEL ROOM R.J. had rented was sparsely furnished with a gaping crack decorating one wall and a cheap print in a plastic frame decorating another. All that was needed was a flashing neon sign outside the window to complete the picture. There was no mark of welcome here, just utility. But it had one advantage: its location. It took seven minutes flat to get to the Richards home. Houston was like that. Angels and devils sometimes lived side by side. The Richardses resided in one of the more exclusive sections of the city, and not a five-minute drive away existence was much more elemental. Poverty endured within the shadows of the vibrant downtown skyline.

Cord lay on the mattress, which felt as if it was stuffed with rocks. He was supposed to be sleeping, but sleep wouldn't come. Precious minutes of his four-hour rest were slipping away.

He turned onto his side and then rolled onto his back. He closed his eyes. It did no good. He still saw her.

He sat up with a curse. Perspiration was bathing his body. The tiny air conditioner in the corner window was having little effect against the heat stored in the room. He raked his hand through his hair.

What the hell was he doing here? Why was he hanging on?

He threw the sheet from his legs and swung his feet to the floor. The cracked linoleum felt cool to the touch. He stood up.

Never in his thirty-eight years had he felt so disconnected. Before the past six months he had always known what he wanted and he had never hesitated to find the means to attain it. At thirteen, when he first learned the truth about his father, he had calculated his escape, never wanting to be beholden to him again. If ever again they met it would be as men on equal terms. One who grasped; one who fought graft.

Later, when in his new life he began to see things that rubbed against those ideals, he had turned his back, justifying, always justifying. Good did sometimes come out of evil, he told himself. Some people had to suffer in order for a goal to be achieved.

Then had come the Wondatta massacre and like a coward he had run. But he couldn't run from himself. Memory played a determined game. Unlike a blackboard, there was no eraser strong enough to wipe away all that he had seen, all that he had done. In himself he saw a part of his father—and that realization terrorized him.

He covered his face with his hands and rocked back on his heels.

He didn't know where he was going now. If he was going...how he was going. Some force outside of himself seemed to be controlling him. It wasn't what R.J. said. He hadn't gone soft on Marlie.

Yet, when he closed his eyes, why couldn't he see anything else? Why, when he awakened, did his thoughts immediately center on her? Why did he feel the need, the urgency, to continue to protect her?

He sank back onto the bed, his strong legs suddenly weak. Each day, when she came outside with her friend or just stood in the doorway in greeting, he watched her as if mesmerized. More often than not he was too far away to hear her voice, or the breeze would carry it away from him. Yet he found himself looking at her like a starving man gazing at a feast that he was not invited to eat. His eyes would follow the familiarity of her every gesture, the sweetness of her infrequent smile. She looked a bit different now, more like the day when he had first seen her. Her clothes were chosen with more care; she wore makeup and did her hair properly.

He remembered kissing her, remembered their quick passion. He moved restlessly on the bed. He didn't like to think about that. It brought up too many other thoughts that did him little good.

In one way it didn't seem as if four days had passed since he had set up guard with R.J. Yet in another, it seemed to be years.

He stretched his length out once again on the lumpy mattress, knowing that he had to rest, knowing that tomorrow would be another hard day.

Why was he still here? he asked himself.

Instinctively he knew the answer, but he shied away from admitting it.

DOYLE JOHNSON FOUND REST to be elusive. In his agitated mind the wrongs committed against him over all his years continued to flow in and out of his consciousness like a gigantic serpentine nightmare.

At times he was afraid that the world wanted to devour him. It had often tried. But he had always escaped. He was too smart. He had known he was smart since he was five years old.

People always paid when they underestimated him. In one way or another, they paid.

Only the world always seemed to be there, ready to catch him when he wasn't aware. That was why he slept so little. Always had to keep a watchful eye.

Sometimes in prison he had felt safe. The world couldn't get through those bars. They were too strong. But the world was strong, too, and sometimes he had to fight ... and fight ... and fight.

William Richards had put him there. Often he forgot exactly why, but the name remained vivid in his mind. William Richards.

Richards had men guarding his house. But guards had never stopped him before. Anyone who could fight against the world and win could do anything.

It wouldn't be long now. He could feel the time approaching. Every part of him was beginning to tingle with anticipation.

He had bought a gun. It had been easy.

He reached across to the nightstand of the seedy hotel room and sighed blissfully when his fingers came into contact with the cold metal.

Not long now at all.

WILLIAM KNEW HE COULD REMAIN sitting on a knife's edge for little longer. Neither could Marlie. He looked across at her, sitting curled on her favorite chair in his study. He had claimed to be attending to a brief and he knew that she had only pretended to want to read a book, because the book was resting unopened on her lap and she was staring off into the distance, focusing on nothing.

He studied her face while she was unaware of him doing so. Lines of strain were beginning to show beside her mouth. She seldom smiled now. And her eyes—there was something more at work in her than fear. In fact, she didn't seem to be afraid. She never spoke of fear unless it was directed to him, for him. The threat seemed to hold no terrors for herself.

William wished that he could slip into her mind and see her thoughts. He had made that same wish more than once over the past few days.

He cleared his throat, drawing her attention, and forced a smile, which she returned fleetingly.

"Not a very interesting book?" he inquired, indicating the unopened novel.

Marlie glanced at it before placing it on the table at her side. "Not particularly."

"I thought it was supposed to be a bestseller."

"It is. It's just...I'm not concentrating very well. It's probably an excellent story. I'm not being fair."

William sighed and closed the folder on his unattended work. "Me, too," he said. "I can't seem to make myself do anything."

"It's this waiting!" Marlie exclaimed, slamming down her fists on the arms of the chair. "I just wish he'd go ahead and get it over with!"

At her show of frustration, William instantly came around his desk to kneel at his daughter's side. "I know. So do I. But there's nothing more we can do."

"Are we going to have to live like this forever? If he decides that we will?"

William could think of nothing more horrible, except an attack that ended in injury.

Marlie's gaze leveled on his own. "What if that's what he wants? What if making us prisoners—afraid to move, afraid to act normally—is what he planned all along? It would be a fair trade-off. He was in prison; we're in prison."

William stood up and paced around the small room. He hadn't thought of that. Was it possible that Doyle Johnson had concocted the entire affair with that very goal in mind? Or was he merely enjoying watching them suffer, drawing out the moment of his revenge? William didn't know what to do. He had made plans for one eventuality but not the other.

Marlie watched her father with hollow eyes. The strain was beginning to tell on her. She wasn't afraid for herself. She couldn't imagine herself dead. She was too young; she had too much of life yet to explore. And sometimes, she wasn't even afraid for her father. Did Doyle Johnson even exist? Or were they caught up in some kind of weird mind game where reality and unreality blended?

She swiveled her gaze to the tightly covered window. The precautions were real. The guards were real. Cord Anderson had been real. The safe house that the two of them had shared in the woods had been real. Unconsciously her fingers touched her mouth and memory swept over her. If she closed her eyes, she could imagine him pulling her against him, his lips plundering her own, her body responding to his. White heat suffused her body.

With a cry, Marlie jumped from the chair, startling herself, startling her father. She stood still, her breath coming in jerky inhalations.

"What is it?" William charged, looking frantically around the room for an intruder.

Marlie rubbed her palms. She felt like such a fool. Her emotions seemed torn in ten different directions and all she wanted was to be held. She rushed into her father's arms. They weren't the right arms, she acknowledged once she was wrapped safely in their protection, but they belonged to her father and she loved him, too.

The import of what she had just thought was hitting Marlie's consciousness when the study door suddenly opened with such force that it hit the connecting wall with a resounding thud.

Both Marlie and her father jumped, clinging to each other in surprise.

A man came into the room, swaggered into the room. Marlie heard her father's gasp of recognition at the same moment as she saw the weapon pointed at them.

For a moment her mind spun. *This can't be happening. Where are the guards?*

CORD HAD TAKEN the early shift that night. R.J. had had to make a couple of calls to Louisiana, so they traded rest periods.

"Nothing's doing as far as I can tell," R.J. had told him. "No one's following him."

"No one's come around here, either."

R.J.'s genial face had broken into a smile. "Do you think this is turning into a wild-goose chase?"

Cord had shaken his head. Something was in the air that night. He could feel it.

"Well, I'm off," his friend had said. "I'll be back around two."

Cord had nodded and narrowed his gaze onto the house while another ripple of awareness shot up his back.

Now, an hour later, Cord was leaning against a slender tree, hidden in the midnight shadow. His movements were slow, calculated . . . when he moved. Most of the time he was perfectly still. Only his eyes and his mind were in motion. He didn't like the feel of this. Something was up. His sense of urgency was growing stronger.

There was no reason for his accentuated caution. He had just completed his perimeter of the house and nothing looked suspicious.

He watched for the guard who usually was stationed in the garden area. He didn't see him. He waited, then looked again.

Without wasting another moment, Cord crept forward, his feet not making a sound. He was in the garden. No one was there. He froze. This wasn't right.

His eyes searched the darkness and settled on a mass heaped against the side of the house some distance from the French doors. He moved quickly, quietly, to its side and reached out. It was one of the guards. He felt the man's neck for a pulse. He was still alive.

Cord squatted at the man's side for another moment, not out of concern but to form a plan. Then, just as quietly, he reached inside his shirt and withdrew his gun. The French doors were closed, secure looking. But when he silently twisted one knob, the door opened. He was inside the house before another breath could be drawn.

Chapter Twelve

"Who are you? What do you want?" Marlie cried, trying to draw the man's attention from her father. The man was staring at William with such evil vindictiveness.

The man spared her only a brief glance. "I think your father can answer that. Can't you, Richards?"

William swallowed. He was afraid that he was going to pass out. His heart was pumping with such vigor that it felt as if it was going to burst.

"I—" he began, only to be cut off.

"You thought you could keep me out," the man said. "Don't you know you can't do that? I've taken care of all your guards. They won't bother us."

Marlie's gaze was riveted on the gun as she clung to her father.

The man waved the weapon in a small circle. "Now, isn't this nice? After all these years."

"Johnson, let me explain." William found his voice.

The gun steadied to a point between them.

"And look at the girl. Did you enjoy your vacation? I saw you get put into the van. I tried to follow you. Thought you might need help. But I got lost."

"Johnson, see here!" William tried to bluff. He also tried to put his body in front of Marlie's, but she would have none of it. She wouldn't allow her life to be saved by his. William cursed her independence.

"I see, Richards. I see more than you know. I see *everything* and everything sees me."

"Doyle...Doyle, put the gun down. Let's talk," William suggested. "I know that I did wrong by you. I wouldn't admit that to myself until... I wouldn't admit it before, but I do now. Let me help you, Doyle. Please. Let me help you."

The mad eyes flickered strangely. "Help me?" he echoed. "Didn't you help me once before?"

Without being aware of it, William's hand tightened to an unbearable degree on Marlie's arm. She wanted to cry out but bit her tongue instead. The man was volatile. Any idiot could see that. All that might be needed to set him off was an unexpected sound.

She looked at him more closely, sensing a vague familiarity, then her memory cleared. He was the man she had seen following her all those days ago. It hadn't been a guard, like Cord had thought or she had thought. It had been Doyle Johnson stalking her. She felt her knees wobble.

If she had described him to her father, he would have known. There was no mistaking the twisted face or the short, stocky body. Passing years had probably resulted in less hair and a lightening of what was left, but they didn't change a nose that looked as if it had been broken one too many times or the disconcerting quality of his stare.

Marlie swallowed and took a step away from her father. He resisted but she would not be denied.

"Mr. Johnson," she said, her voice husky, "why don't you sit down so that we can talk this over. I don't believe you want to hurt us."

"What makes you think that?" he asked. The dead way he asked the question did little to reassure Marlie. But at least she had his attention now.

She forced a smile. "Would you like some coffee? Something to eat? You look as if you might be hungry."

The smile he flashed at her caused Marlie's blood to curdle. She had never seen such insane malevolence.

"I'm hungry, all right. I've waited years for this. You know, I used to stay awake nights—I don't like to sleep very much—just thinking about you, Richards. And I read the papers. I saw you, your daughter. Marlie…isn't that her name? It's a pretty name. Real pretty. Just like she is."

William took an angry step forward. "Leave her out of this!" he thundered.

Doyle Johnson smiled again. "I think I'll kill her first."

The gun swiveled toward Marlie. She caught her breath. Death suddenly seemed very real to her; no longer was it bathed in impossibility. The hollow bore of the pistol looked enormous. She saw his finger tighten on the trigger.

Then the picture before her blurred. There was movement from the corner of her eye and a gunshot shattered the still air. Almost immediately her father made a small sound and crumpled to the floor.

For a moment, Marlie was unable to comprehend what was happening. Then she saw Cord—Cord!—wrestling with Doyle Johnson.

Both men were struggling for possession of Johnson's gun. Cord was the larger of the two but dementia added to his adversary's strength. Cord's own gun had fallen to the carpet. Marlie recognized it from the safe house.

As if in a dream, she stepped forward to retrieve it, holding the weapon unfamiliarly in her hand. It felt cold and heavy and lethal. There was no question of her firing it at the moment, even if she knew how. She looked up at the two men, her heart leaping into her throat as Johnson twisted away from Cord's hold. Cord quickly lunged after him, though, throwing his weight against him. The lamp on the desk was knocked to the floor. The skier and Monica's picture soon followed. Cord managed to pin Johnson to the desk top.

"Run! Get out!" he yelled at her, his words tense, sharp. Doyle Johnson was fighting like a street brawler, using his knees, trying to use his teeth. The two men struggled for another moment then dropped to the floor.

Marlie didn't move. She couldn't. Her body seemed petrified by fear—for Cord, for herself, for her father. She dragged her eyes away from the men to find her father. He wasn't moving and there was a pool of blood staining the carpet beneath him.

Marlie drew a halting breath. Was he dead? She shook her head, denying it.

Doyle Johnson started to curse. At the top of his lungs he screeched every foul word that he had ever learned. Then, with one mighty shove, he threw Cord off of him, only to scuttle across the floor to retrieve the gun that had fallen there. Before her horrified gaze, he grasped it, steadied it and aimed for Cord's heart.

Marlie started to tremble uncontrollably. She heard a keening sound but she wasn't aware that the noise was coming from her. Neither was she aware that she had lifted Cord's gun until suddenly it was there, in place, and smoke was erupting from the barrel. At the same instant another explosion sounded in the room, the two loud cracks blending into one.

The silence that followed was deafening. Tears swam before Marlie's eyes. She stared at the gun in her hand, unable to believe that she had fired it, unable to believe all that had happened. Her trembling increased as she saw Doyle Johnson lying motionless on the floor.

From that point everything seemed to happen in slow motion. She saw that Cord was holding his side and that blood was spreading out to stain his shirt beneath his fingers. He knelt beside Doyle Johnson, moving to the man's head, turning it so that he could examine the wound.

Marlie closed her eyes, not wanting to see. The gun clattered to the floor from her lifeless fingers.

"He's alive," Cord said. "Just knocked out. The bullet grazed his head." He stepped to the drapes and pulled one tieback from its holder. He used the cord to secure the man so that when he regained consciousness he would pose no further danger. The patch of blood on Cord's shirt was growing larger, but he seemed not to notice that he was wounded.

When he was done with his chore, his eyes settled on Marlie. "Are you all right?"

Marlie was cold, so cold, but she managed to nod her head yes.

Cord hurried to her father's side. With care, he examined the wound. "I think we'd better get an ambulance. This doesn't look good."

At that moment one of the security guards staggered into the room. He was dazed but he evaluated the scene rapidly. When he saw Cord kneeling over his employer, he reached for his gun but found the holster was empty. Consternation crossed his face. He took a step forward, ready to do battle without a weapon.

When Marlie saw what he was preparing to do, she cried for him to stop. He had no idea that Cord had helped them. For all he knew, he might be the killer. "No, he's one of us. It's okay. It's...okay."

The guard pulled up short as Cord straightened. "Call an ambulance," he directed the man. "Hurry."

Marlie moved to the chair she had been sitting in earlier and lowered herself to a seat. If she didn't sit down she might fall and all they needed right then was another person lying on the floor. A haze had engulfed her mind, carrying in shock and disbelief. Then slowly it began to clear and with an anguished sob she threw herself to her father's side.

How much time passed after that, she didn't know. But soon she was being pulled away. She lifted her head to gaze up at Cord, who had helped her to her feet. His features were cold, shuttered.

"Cord?" she breathed his name in bewilderment. "Why are you here?"

Voices sounded in the hallway, strengthening as they moved into the room. The study seemed to fill rapidly—with police, with ambulance technicians, with Regina and her parents, who were standing in their robes looking shattered by what had transpired.

A paramedic bent to his knees at her father's side while another began to examine Doyle Johnson. Regina moved closer to Marlie. She called her name softly, not unaware of the stranger who was holding her friend. She met the man's gaze and instinctively knew that he was the man Marlie had told her about. How he had come to be here, and why, when he had been dismissed, was a question for another time. Yet, without reason, she trusted him.

Marlie was passed from one to the other.

"Take care of her," Cord directed before he moved to talk with the police officer and the security guard who had gathered at the doorway.

Marlie returned her friend's gaze with bruised eyes. Regina made a solicitous sound and gathered her to her breast.

"We heard gunshots. At first we thought it was something else—a car backfiring or something. But when we heard the sirens..."

"It was him," Marlie whispered, pointing to Doyle Johnson, who had regained consciousness and was struggling against his binding.

"Who is he?" Regina asked. "Is he the man who...?"

"Excuse me," murmured a paramedic. Her father had been placed on a gurney and was being wheeled toward the door.

Marlie covered her mouth with her hand. She and Regina moved out of the way.

"I want to go with him," she told the room.

The paramedic glanced at the police officer who seemed to be in charge of the other policemen who had answered the call. He nodded shortly. "Let her go. We'll talk to her at the hospital."

Marlie started to follow but paused to glance at Cord. "What about you?" she asked.

"What about me?" he countered.

"You're hurt, too."

One of the paramedics noticed the blood on Cord's shirt and demanded that he be allowed to examine him.

"You need to come along, too," he said after a moment.

Cord's jaw tightened. "I'm all right."

"Officer?"

The policeman narrowed his eyes. "Go along. We'll take your statement at the hospital when we take Miss Richards's."

Cord looked as if he were about to protest once again but in the end, he acquiesced. He followed Marlie and Regina to the ambulance parked in the long drive. They waited while William was settled into place, his temporary lifeline secured, the paramedic at his side.

Marlie turned to Regina. "Would you come, too?" she asked. Regina was family, as near to a sister as she would ever have.

Regina shook her head. "There isn't room in there for all of us. My parents and I will get dressed and follow in our car."

Marlie nodded woodenly. Cord took her elbow and helped her into the vehicle, then he stepped in behind her.

The rear of the ambulance was crowded and the trip to the hospital was a nightmare. Lights flashed while the siren screamed. All the while the attendant worked on her father and examined Cord more fully.

One hour ago she and her father had been sitting in the study. Everything had been quiet. Little more than a half hour ago she had wished out loud that Doyle Johnson would get it over with.

Marlie bit her bottom lip in an attempt to keep it from trembling. Quiet tears rolled over her cheeks. Her father was still unconscious. Would he wake up? He had to. He *had* to!

Her gaze moved to Cord, whom the paramedic had forced to stretch out on a narrow cushioned ledge. When she looked at him it was to discover that he was already looking at her.

She wiped her tears away with the back of her hand. There was so much she wanted to say to him, to ask him—not least of which was how badly he was hurt. She knew him; he wouldn't admit to pain. He would have to be unconscious before he would allow anyone to see any weakness. But the words wouldn't come and she wasn't sure that he would answer if they had.

The ambulance swung into the hospital drive and stopped at the doors to the emergency room. The attendants jumped out, quickly, efficiently, not wasting a moment or a movement. Her father was withdrawn first, Cord second. She stood at the rear of the vehicle feeling helpless.

Her helplessness didn't decrease when the group entered the hospital proper. Nurses came, doctors followed. Her father was sent to one examining room while Cord went to another. She was told to wait.

Other people were in the waiting room, some suffering from various ailments, some not. Most had hollow eyes. She knew that she did. So much had happened so quickly. The smell of disinfectant assailed her nostrils, turning her stomach.

She sat on a hard plastic chair molded into a curving seat and chair back. She didn't notice the discomfort.

When Regina and her parents arrived a short time later, Marlie rushed to meet them. Until then she had felt so alone.

"Have you heard anything yet?" Regina asked, strain showing on her round face.

"Not yet," Marlie answered.

James Campo glanced over his shoulder at the nurses' station. "I'll see if I can find out anything." He moved away.

The women chose seats close together.

"I just can't believe this," Barbara Campo murmured. "It doesn't seem real!"

Regina clasped Marlie's hand.

They sat in silence for a short time before Regina's father returned. A nurse followed closely behind him.

"Miss Richards?" she asked.

Marlie sat forward, a knot of apprehension in her throat.

"Your father is conscious now," the nurse said. "I was just coming to find you when Mr.—" She caught herself. "Your father is going to require surgery. Would you come with me, please?"

Marlie's legs felt numb as she followed the nurse. She knew that the Campos' commiseration came with her.

When the two of them passed the door to the room where Cord had been taken, she asked, "What about Mr. Anderson? Is he—"

"The doctor is with him now. This way, please."

Marlie hesitated for a second before following her into the next room. She wanted to be with both men.

Her father was pale, his face drawn. But he was awake. "Marlie..." he whispered fiercely, groping for her hand.

She hurried to his side. "I'm here." Her voice was thick with emotion.

"What happened? I thought...I thought Johnson was going to...kill you."

Marlie's fingers trembled as they smoothed strands of silver hair away from her father's forehead. "He was, but Cord stopped him. The bullet hit you instead."

"I don't remember—" William broke off. His mind was fuzzy. He was having trouble staying awake. "What...what was Cord...?"

"I don't know. He just...appeared."

An attendant came into the room. Marlie glanced at him and then at her father. She didn't want him to be taken away, but she knew that he had to be in order to be helped. "Dad—I love you, Dad!"

Her father's fingers tightened in response to the terror he heard behind her words. "Don't worry, honey. I'll be all right, I promise."

After the attendant finished preparing the gurney to be moved, he waited for her to step aside.

Marlie saw her father through a blur of tears as he was wheeled past her. She tried to smile but she wasn't sure if she succeeded.

She followed them into the hall and was just in time to see the door to the next examination room open and a man in a white jacket emerge. He was frowning down at the clipboard that he held in his hand.

"Doctor?" she called, gaining his attention. "How is he?"

His eyes narrowed. "Are you Miss Richards?"

She nodded.

The doctor glanced at the gurney moving down the hallway. "The surgery's going to be delicate but we're calling in our best man. I'm sure Dr. Page will speak with you before..."

Marlie nodded, cutting him off. "And Mr. Anderson?" When she had asked the previous question, she had been referring to Cord, not her father, but she didn't correct the mistaken impression with the doctor.

"It's a flesh wound. A lot of bleeding but little damage. A few stitches should put him right."

The policeman who had been in her house arrived at that moment. He conferred with the doctor before speaking to Marlie. "I'll question you shortly, Miss Richards, if that will be satisfactory. I understand you'll be in the surgical waiting room?" He turned back to the doctor before Marlie could reply. "Now, where is Mr. Anderson? If it's possible I'd like to take his statement now."

The doctor indicated the door behind them and the policeman went inside. In the seconds that the door was open, Marlie saw that Cord was sitting up, stripped to the waist, holding a square of white gauze to his side.

He looked up and their eyes met before the door swung shut.

Marlie stifled a cry. She wanted to go to Cord, to talk with him, to ask him why he hadn't gone away even though her father had dismissed him. He had stayed. Why? What did it mean?

The elevator doors at the end of the hall swished open and Marlie saw the attendant push her father inside. Then he looked back at her and held the door, silently asking if she wished to accompany them.

Marlie was torn in two. Through everything that had happened, she hadn't forgotten the discovery she'd made before Doyle Johnson burst into the study. She loved Cord. She didn't know how or why or when it had happened. But it had.

The attendant removed his hand from the door stop, obviously unwilling to wait any longer for her decision. He had a job to do and he wasn't going to be delayed in doing it.

Marlie sprang forward. Her father was injured more seriously than Cord. The operation was going to be delicate. And at his age...and after having faced such trauma...

Marlie stepped into the elevator just before the doors clamped shut. From the corner of her eye she saw her father reach out to her from beneath the sheet that covered him. She swallowed tightly as she met his hand halfway.

Chapter Thirteen

Cord drew a shallow breath as he stepped through the swinging doors that exited the emergency room. Anything more reminded him that he had been shot. He had called R.J. and told him what had happened and also asked to be picked up. He looked around the parking area. When he saw that his friend had not yet arrived, he took up a waiting position against the side of the building.

It was at times like these that he wished he smoked, since smoking would give him something to do besides think.

He shifted to a more comfortable position then soon shifted again. The night was lighted like day near the hospital. Bugs buzzed around the tall lamps in a frenzy of fascination. Cord watched them and wondered if an observer would think that he had acted just as witlessly.

The man had gotten by him. Somehow…some way. He had knocked out the other guards, which didn't surprise him, and entered the house. He had almost killed Marlie.

Cord remembered that moment. The weapon he had drawn in readiness had been useless. If he had fired, hitting him, the man's finger would have squeezed reflexively on the trigger, finishing in death what he had begun in life. He had been left with only one option. And William Richards had paid the price.

Cord shifted position again, wishing that R.J. would hurry up. A moment later his wait was rewarded. He recognized his friend's car and moved to the curb.

The passenger door was swung open almost as soon as the car came to a stop.

"I'm sorry I missed the show," R.J. said as Cord settled into the seat.

"It wasn't very pretty."

"No—" R.J. examined him through narrowed eyes. "You okay?"

"Of course."

"How's the father?"

"He's in surgery right now. Let's go, huh?"

"What's your hurry?" R.J. asked even as he set the car in motion.

Cord didn't answer.

"What happened with the girl?" R.J. asked. "She get hurt?"

"No."

"Did she thank you for staying on?"

"No."

The succinct answer raised R.J.'s eyebrows.

"She was worried about her father," Cord excused.

R.J. grunted, not making a comment. Finally he asked, "You going to have to hang around here for a bit?"

"The police advised me to, until all the loose ends are tied up."

R.J. laughed. "Yeah, I like the way they sometimes *advise*." He glanced at Cord. "I was thinking that maybe you'd come to Louisiana for a time. I have an extra room."

"I don't know what I'm going to do."

R.J. was silent a moment. "You thinking about quitting, too?"

Cord knew what he was referring to without the words being said. "Maybe," he answered.

For a time only the car's engine sounded in their ears. When they drew into the motel's parking area, R.J. said, "I haven't regretted it. Not for a minute."

In spite of himself Cord thought of Marlie and what he had almost let himself believe when they had been together. It could never be. Seeing her in her fine home, seeing how much she loved her father, had made him realize that if nothing else had. William Richards would never stand for a close relationship between the two of them even if she would.

He was glad that he had stayed, though, even if other eyes might think him foolish. He had saved Marlie, and hopefully he had also saved William. He had done everything that he could be expected to do. The job was truly over now. Once the police released him, he would go away. Only to where?

The car had stopped and R.J. was stepping out. "Just remember the room," he reminded. "It's yours any time you want it."

"I'll remember that," Cord murmured as he, too, stepped outside. He reached into his back pocket. "Here. Let me pay you for your time. Will this do?" He held out a grouping of bills.

R.J. shook his head. "No. I won't take it. This is a repayment. And I still owe you one."

"You don't owe me anything."

"I say I do."

Cord saw the resolution in R.J.'s face. He shrugged then held out his hand.

R.J. took it in past and future friendship.

HAVING TO RELIVE the terrible moments was an ordeal for Marlie but once it was over, the police sergeant seemed satisfied.

"You won't be leaving town in the next few days, will you?" he asked. Marlie reassured him that she wouldn't. That seemed to satisfy him, too. As an afterthought, he wished her father a speedy recovery. Marlie wondered if that was so that he could question him, as well.

When the policeman left, Marlie resumed her seat. The Campos were with her. She fidgeted a short time before restlessly getting to her feet. She was worried about her father; she was worried about Cord.

She turned to Regina. "I—I have to go downstairs for a bit. Will you . . . ?"

"We won't move. If someone comes out, we'll be right here."

Marlie gave her friend a grateful hug and hurried to the elevator. Not too much time had passed. She hoped he would still be there.

As she rode down to the ground floor Marlie wondered what she would say to him. How could she possibly thank him for what he had done?

When she arrived in the emergency area, she walked directly toward the examining room where she had last seen Cord. But before she got very far down the hall, one of the nurses stopped her.

"Yes? May I help you?" she said in the way that informs a person that he has no business being where he is.

Marlie caught the tone and motioned toward the door. "I wanted to see Mr. Anderson."

The nurse looked blankly at her for a moment before saying, "He's already gone."

"He's gone?" Marlie repeated.

"About ten minutes ago."

"But . . ."

"He asked about your father."

"He did?"

"We told him we had no information—which we don't."

"No…" Marlie murmured, her mind adrift. He was gone. Where did he go? "Did, ah, did he leave a message?"

"None that I know of, but then we're not a secretarial service."

Marlie didn't take the hint. "You said he left ten minutes ago?"

The nurse sighed with exasperation. "I wasn't looking at my watch."

Marlie glanced at the swing doors at the end of the hall that led outside. She might be able to catch him. Stranger things had happened.

"Thank you," she murmured before hurrying away.

Outside, another ambulance was backing into place and the attendants were jumping out. She stepped aside, turning her face from the accident victim. She had seen all the blood she could handle for one day. She didn't know how the hospital personnel did it day after day, night after night.

She hurried into the parking lot. If he had called a taxi, he might still be waiting for it, but he was not standing where she could see him. Maybe he was farther toward the street.

Her search was futile; he was nowhere to be found. She even walked to the front of the hospital, hoping that he might be there. But he was not.

Marlie retraced her steps, unconsciously acknowledging the fact that she only knew one way to the surgical wing and that was through the emergency entrance. She didn't think to use another.

No one questioned her as she moved through the swing doors or walked down the hall to the elevator. And she might not have answered if they had tried.

She was aware of only one thing: for the second time in a week Cord had walked out of her life. And this time she might not ever see him again.

Why had he stayed? To have arrived so swiftly, he must have been watching the house. Why? To protect her? To protect her father? But her father had dismissed him. It didn't make any sense. Unless . . .

Marlie stopped short. Lightning might have struck her. Unless . . . she thought wondrously, he had come to the same realization as she.

She hadn't recognized her feelings before this night. She knew that she had been attracted to him. Any woman would, he was that sort of man. But love?

Yes, she loved him. That was why she cared so very much that he not blame himself for his past. That he not let it tear him apart. When she had pushed him to talk, when she had responded to his kisses, to his silences, to his voice, it had been the forerunner to a much deeper feeling than fascination. She loved him.

Was it possible that he had come to feel something for her? Any feeling would be monumental for him. Cord held himself very closely to himself. At first he had been impenetrable. Then he had begun to trust her; she knew that he had. Otherwise...

Otherwise she would not have been able to get away.

The elevator came and she stepped inside. With automatic action, she pushed the correct floor button. Her thoughts continued, only now they weren't so positive.

She had escaped. She had used his trust. He had told her things about himself that she suspected he had told no one before. And she had used that special trust against him. He had treated her like ice in her father's office. And she had taken her father's side. Against him. And today, when he was hurt—after having saved them both—she hadn't even taken the time to talk to him. To him, it probably looked as if she didn't care. As if she was ungrateful for all that he had done. As if she accepted his sacrifice as their due.

Marlie's moan of despair echoed hollowly in the tiny cubicle.

CORD LEFT THE DINGY ROOM he had rented the night before in the same motel where R.J. was staying. The hour had been late upon their arrival and his side had been aching more than he cared to acknowledge. So rather than find a new place, one that was cleaner and cooler, he had stayed there.

R.J. was standing beside a dented soft-drink machine. He smiled when he saw Cord. "I wasn't sure I'd see you before I left."

"The beds in this place don't exactly invite a person to linger."

R.J. laughed. "We've both seen worse."

"You're right, but we didn't have to pay."

His friend gave him an all-encompassing look. Then abruptly he said, "Why don't you try to work things out with her?"

"Who?" Cord pretended ignorance.

"That girl. I think you're ready to settle down, Cord. I can see the signs. You're more like me than the others. You can take that life, but you can leave it better. Why don't you do it? Stay here, see what you can work out."

"If I quit, it won't be to stay here."

"Why not?"

Cord didn't answer.

R.J. waited several seconds. "Don't keep screwing up your life, kid. I'm older than you and I wish I had quit at your age."

"I'll have to think about it," Cord murmured obstinately.

R.J. pretended to cuff him on the ear. "If you ever need me again, call. I'll come running."

"The same goes for me."

R.J. nodded. Then he got in his car and drove away.

Cord's fingers tightened on the straps of his duffel bag. He still had the van, the one he had abducted Marlie in, the one in which he had raced back to Houston. At first he had thought to get rid of it immediately. Now he decided to hang on to it for a time.

He climbed into the driver's seat and set off to find a new hotel room.

WILLIAM CAME to fuzzy awareness of his strange surroundings. It wasn't his room at home. It looked... He was in the hospital. When he tried to sit up, hands immediately stopped him.

Marlie's sweet face was smiling down at him. "You can't get up, Dad. You're wired."

William frowned. Wired? Then he moved his head enough so that he could see the trail of tubes that extended from his body. It wasn't exactly a reassuring sight.

Marlie must have seen his shock because she hurriedly said, "It's okay. You're fine. They tell me they'll be taking these out in a couple of days."

William's head fell back to the pillow. "What happened?" he asked weakly. "I don't—" With those words, memory returned. "Yes, I do. Johnson!"

"He's in jail. We don't have to worry about him anymore."

William closed his eyes. He would always worry about him and not just because he had tried to carry out his threat. He was going to help him. The vow he had taken when he was worried and frightened had not been made in vain. Whatever it took, he would do it, until justice had been worked for the man—whether it meant the best in mental treatment, or physical aid. He couldn't continue to live with himself if he did less.

Marlie started to move away from the bed, back to the chair she had occupied for the past day. She thought her father had fallen asleep again. He had awakened slightly several times recently, but this was the first time that he had been coherent. She was wondering if she should call the nurse to tell her he had spoken when his voice interrupted her plan.

"Anderson. Did I see him?"

Marlie was slow in answering. "Yes. He saved our lives."

William frowned. "But why?"

"I don't know. I didn't get to speak with him."

William's frown deepened. He wanted to ask something else, but the question became elusive. He suddenly fell back to sleep.

Marlie resettled in the chair. She had been thinking about Cord constantly. How could she find him? Where might he be?

Her only consolation was the assurance she'd had to give the police sergeant that she would be available for the next few days. Cord would have had to do the same. So that meant he was somewhere in Houston. He had to be. Only that brought her back to the original question: how could she find him?

As time passed, her need to see him had grown. With each hourly improvement in her father's condition, the more her mind switched from her concern for him to her concern for Cord. She didn't want Cord to think that she didn't care. Not even if she was wrong in her speculation and he felt nothing for her in the least.

An idea suddenly occurred to her. The sergeant. He would know where Cord was. Maybe he would tell her. She reached for the telephone and talked softly so that she wouldn't disturb her father.

She was wrong. The Sphinx had nothing on the policeman. He was a sponge for information, but getting any back was impossible.

She sat down again and waited, her mind restlessly moving from option to option.

WILLIAM AWAKENED AGAIN a few hours later. Shortly afterward the surgeon came into the room to examine him. "Coming along nicely," he pronounced. When the doctor left, Marlie slipped back into position by his side.

The smile she gave him in return to his own game offering was fleeting and he wasn't too weak or too fuzzy-minded to realize that something was wrong.

As she sat down after kissing his forehead, he asked, "What is it, sweetheart?"

Marlie didn't want to tell him. He had enough problems just regaining strength. But he wouldn't let the matter rest and she finally gave in. It was either that or have him wear himself out questioning her. And he was a fairly good questioner, considering his occupation.

"I want to find Cord, Dad."

"Why?"

Marlie looked at her hands. "To thank him."

William studied his daughter. "What else?"

The softly worded question caused Marlie's head to snap up. They exchanged a long look.

"What happened while you were away, Marlie?"

She didn't try to evade the question. Evasions and half-truths never worked for very long. And if for some reason they did, their complications were always magnified. Wasn't that what had happened to both Cord and her father? "I think I fell in love with him," she answered simply.

William wished that this revelation had come at another time. He felt so powerless lying in bed, his body a wounded mass. He strove to remain calm.

"This is something you need to be very sure about," he advised.

"I am sure."

"But you've only known him for a couple of weeks."

"I can't help that."

William shifted position, uncomfortably aware that his pain medication was wearing off. "What about him? Does he love you, too? Is that why he stayed on the job?"

Marlie looked at her hands again. "I don't know." She knew that her father was hurting and that what she had told him had upset him. "I didn't want to tell you this now. I don't want to worry you. But . . ."

"But you want to find him, and you don't know how. Is that right?"

Marlie bit her bottom lip. She nodded.

William gazed at her bent head, his love for her forcing him to swallow any further protest he might want to make. He didn't want to lose her to another man. He had watched over her for so long, protecting her, keeping her safe. Yet all along he had known the day would come.

He cleared his throat and winced from the action. "He's still in town, wouldn't you think?"

Marlie met his gaze. The ball of tension that had knotted her stomach began to loosen. Her father understood.

William saw hope spring into her eyes. If he'd had a hand in picking the man Marlie fell in love with, it wouldn't have been Cord Anderson. He was too hard, too worldly-wise, too cynical.

"I'm sure the police have asked him to stay for a few days," she said.

William nodded. "Would you like me to see what I can find out?"

A flash of excitement lighted her face and then just as quickly disappeared. "I don't think you're up to this now."

"I'm up to what I want to be up to. Hand me the phone."

"Dad, are you sure?"

"You want to find him, don't you?"

"Yes."

"Then hand me the phone."

"Tell me the number and I'll dial it."

William thought for a moment. He had contacts on both the district attorney's staff and in the police department. He chose one and reeled off the number. Soon he would have to ask for more medication and he wanted to get this over with before he did.

MARLIE APPROACHED THE HOTEL. It was one she had been to frequently while attending various social functions. She stepped through the wide front doors into the familiar lobby.

She was nervous. As nervous as she had ever been. She didn't know if she was doing the right thing. What if he told her to get lost? What if he continued to look at her in that icy manner? Would she have the fortitude to carry on? Exactly what was it that she wanted from him?

She knew what room he was staying in. There was no need to check at the desk.

She slipped into the ladies' room, ostensibly to check her appearance. The wind had been howling through the caverns created by the downtown buildings and her hair had blown this way and that.

As she attempted to tame it, she stared at herself in the mirror. Huge eyes looked back at her from a face that was unnaturally pale.

She could leave. He would never know that she had attempted to see him. Only... Only then *she* would never know.

Marlie slipped the comb back into her purse and consciously squared her shoulders.

He probably wouldn't be overwhelmed to see her. She had to be prepared for that, if he agreed to talk to her at all.

During the elevator ride to the tenth floor her tension mounted. This situation was so different from their meetings before. In each, he had been the catalyst: he had abducted her, he had rushed into the room to save her from Doyle Johnson. Now she was the one making the move.

The distance from the elevator to his room was short, too short for her to do anything more to collect herself. Her hand felt clammy as she balled it into a fist and knocked.

She waited for his answer with a pounding heart.

Chapter Fourteen

A small gasp escaped Marlie's lips when the door was pulled open. She couldn't help it. The action was involuntary. But she would have given much not to have done it. She needed every scrap of confidence that she could muster.

His expression didn't change as he registered who his visitor was. He looked just as cold and hard as she remembered him from the beginning of their acquaintance. Any softening in him in the past might have been a figment of her imagination, for all the evidence he gave.

Marlie's face felt frozen but she managed a small smile. "Are you surprised?" she asked. There was a slight quiver in her voice but nothing to give away the cataclysmic quaking going on inside her.

His pale eyes flickered over her face. "What about?" he asked.

She had known that this was not going to be easy. "To see me," she replied. "I thought you might be surprised."

"How did you find me? The police?"

Marlie nodded. "I—I wanted to thank you...for what you did."

He merely looked at her.

Her fingers tightened on her purse. "My father's out of danger now."

"Good."

A tiny muscle jumped at the side of Marlie's mouth. "How are you? I mean...your side."

"It was just a scratch."

"It was more than that."

He shrugged.

The wall he lived behind seemed to have grown bigger than before. Marlie knew that if she turned away at that moment, he would not try to stop her. No matter what he might feel.

She ducked under the arm he had placed across the doorway in silent protest to her entry and slipped inside the room. She looked around, trying to pretend that she was welcome. "Nice. I didn't expect to find you in a place like this."

He closed the door and leaned against it, his arms folded across his chest, his handsome face cut from stone. There was no welcome for her feat, no amusement. "I like a little luxury once in a while."

"I see," she said, trying to form her thoughts. When she looked at him, standing there so familiarly in his jeans and plaid shirt, she couldn't help but remember the time they had spent in the safe house, the times his reserve had been swept away, both in conversation and in passion. She wanted to ignore the differences that separated them and rush into his arms. She ached to feel them around her once again. She wanted his kisses, his touch.

Was it possible to fall in love with so little encouragement? Yes, because she had. But then maybe she didn't need much prompting. Maybe she sensed that behind his reserve was a wealth of emotion that needed an outlet. An outlet that was herself. She wasn't the personality type to cling to a dream, to make reality out of unreality. What had passed between them had not been one-sided.

Her glance skimmed over the king-size bed and settled on one of two chairs arranged on either side of a small table. "May I sit down?"

"If you must."

Marlie ignored his sarcasm. She settled in the chair. "I suppose the police asked you to stay in town until they cleared everything up?"

"You suppose right."

"How long do you think that will take?"

"I have no idea."

"A day or two more?" she asked.

"You have better contacts with them than I do."

"Why don't you sit down?"

"I'm fine where I am."

"Are you afraid of me?" She made a direct attack. He said nothing.

Marlie shifted in her chair, retreating. "What are you going to do afterward?"

"Why do you ask?"

"I'm interested."

He pushed away from the door. She watched as he took up his usual position by a window. When he didn't answer her question, an alarming thought occurred to her.

"You're not going back to fighting, are you?"

"I may."

She felt a knot tighten in her stomach. "But you can't. You said—"

"I said a lot of things. Too many things."

"No!" Marlie jumped to her feet.

He glanced at her and then away again. "What I do is no business of yours."

"I think it is."

"Then you think wrong."

Marlie no longer restrained herself. She ran to his side. "Cord, no...you can't do that! You hate that life. Remember the little girl? Remember what you said? It's not right for you. Not right at all."

He pushed her hand away only to have it return. "Please, Cord..."

He jerked away. "Stop playing games, Marlie."

"I'm not," she denied. "It's you who likes to play games. Little boy games where people get hurt."

"Then they shouldn't get in the way."

Marlie was repelled by the callousness. "You don't think that. I know you don't. Stop being so...so hard!"

His pale eyes glittered as he swung around to look at her. If she hadn't known him better, she would be afraid. But she did know him. And she had to fight for him. For both of them.

His hands darted out to give her a jolting shake as he rasped, "When are you going to realize that I *am* a hard man? Find someone else to lay your fantasies on, Marlie. Don't put them on me. I'd just as soon kill a person as look at them."

Tears came into her eyes but she batted them away. "Then why did you stay in Houston? If you're such a terrible person, why did you stay?"

"Temporary insanity."

He released her to put some distance between them.

Marlie drew a shuddering breath. He was doing his best to discourage her and his method was beginning to work. Not that she believed him. He was not as bad a person as he made himself out to be. But to realize that he would go to such lengths of dissuasion hurt her, hurt her deeply.

"You saved my life, Cord."

He shrugged.

"You saved my father's life, as well."

"I practically got your father killed."

"If you hadn't come when you did, we both would be dead. What happened to my father was an accident."

"Tell him to hire better guards next time."

"There won't be a next time."

"Lucky you."

She was silent a moment, then she said quietly, "Do you *want* to die, Cord? Is that why you're going back to that kind of life?"

"I could die crossing a city street."

"Then why not stay here and take your chances like the rest of us?"

"Maybe I crave adventure."

"Then I crave adventure, too. Take me with you."

Her request jolted him. His head snapped up. "You?"

The way he said the word made her cringe. If he felt that way about her, there was little use in her carrying on. But stubbornly, she lifted her chin and said, "Why not? Aren't there any women mercenaries?"

His mouth twisted. "Not like you."

"What's the matter with me? You think I wouldn't be able to keep up?"

"Remember what happened that time at the house? You wouldn't last a minute."

"I got away from you."

Maybe she shouldn't have said that, but she had to break through to him. To pursue the subject, she asked, "What's the matter? Did my escape hurt your macho image of yourself? Do you think you're so very perfect?"

"No, I don't think I'm perfect."

"Then take me with you."

"Stop being silly."

"Why is it silly when I want to go, but not silly when you do? We can die together. Wouldn't that be fun?"

"Marlie, stop it!" He was angry, his body tense.

She didn't pay attention to his directive. "I can see our tombstones now: 'one who knew too much' and 'one who knew too little.' There, don't you think that's good?"

"I said stop it!"

Again she paid him no heed. "But maybe before we pay the final price, we can come upon some innocent villagers and wipe them out. You know how they get in the way. Always standing there so helpless."

He crossed the distance that separated them in two quick strides. "Don't talk like that," he grated dangerously, jerking her around and holding her face inches from his own. "I don't like to hear you talk that way."

Marlie defied him. "Why not?" she challenged. "You said yourself..."

She felt the shudder that passed through his body. It was a quake that registered with equal intensity in her own.

She became very still. The wall he had reinforced around himself was cracking. "Why, Cord?" she repeated. The moment of truth had come.

When he still refused to answer, Marlie supplied softly, with infinite gentleness, "Because you care for me?"

Cord closed his eyes. From the time she appeared at his door, he had been trying to avoid this moment. He knew he loved her. But that wasn't good enough. She deserved someone as innocent of the world as she was. She deserved someone who would be able to continue to provide the sheltered, wealthy life that she was accustomed to living. He could fulfill neither of those requirements.

"Go away from here, Marlie. Forget about me. Forget about everything that's happened."

"No," Marlie answered steadfastly.

Cord gazed at her sweet face, at the tenderness in her eyes. "I'm not the right man for you. Ask your friend. Ask your father."

"I'm the only one whose opinion counts. And I think you are."

She reached out to touch his face, her fingers moving along the side of his cheek.

Her touch, her look, was battering down Cord's resistance. How much longer could he hold out in opposition to such determination?

Her lips curved into a soft smile and that action was his undoing. He had tried to hold himself aloof. He had been trying ever since their return to Houston. But it had done him little good.

He gave a low groan and wound his fingers in her hair. Then he slowly directed her mouth toward his, giving her a chance to change her mind. Yet he knew, deep inside himself, that he would never let her pull away.

He had been afraid, of her, of what she might do to his life. He had known that if he allowed himself to fall completely under her influence everything would change. And he wasn't sure that he could handle more change. Enough was going on that he had to resolve. Falling in love was out of the question. And yet loving her had come upon him with such little fanfare.

Marlie's eyes fluttered shut. If she continued to look at him, she thought that she might faint. All she wanted was to feel his lips against hers, feel the breakthrough that meant he cared.

He might love her; he might not. But at this stage in their relationship any show of emotion would be held dear.

She waited, but the kiss never came. Seconds passed, still there was no contact. Her eyes slowly opened. His face was near, but it came no nearer.

Marlie smiled tremulously, trying to cover her unease, her confusion.

"What's the matter?" she whispered. "I know you haven't forgotten how."

Cord smoothed her hair. More long seconds passed—seconds during which the tortured look on his face magnified. Then he said softly, "The answer is still no."

Marlie's smile faded. She didn't understand. She knew he wanted her and she would gamble everything she owned that he loved her as well. She searched his face, looking for a clue.

It was all Cord could do not to drag her back against him and never let her go. He wanted to do that more than he wanted life itself. But years of discipline helped him control his desires. One of them had to be responsible.

"I didn't mean really *go* with you," she said, stumbling. "Not to...wherever it is you were thinking about going. I thought..."

Her words were barely coherent, but Cord understood. He interrupted their flow. "This has happened pretty fast, Marlie. I believe we both need time to step back and look at it."

Marlie took a few seconds to collect herself. Then her eyes flashed. "So you admit that *something* has happened?"

Cord retained her gaze. "I admit it."

"But not what."

"You're very young. Not so much in years but in outlook. You've been protected, coddled."

"I know what I feel, Cord. I love you."

"Maybe you only think that you do."

Marlie stepped away from him, anger and hurt blending with the sting of rejection. "What, exactly, do you feel for me? Or are you going to deny that you feel anything?"

"I'm not a liar. I feel something."

Once, even moments before, she would have been satisfied with that. Now she needed more. She *had* to have more. "Something?" she challenged. "That word again. Define something."

Cord wouldn't be drawn. Instead he said quietly, "What's been happening in your life over the past few weeks is out of the ordinary. At the safe house you identified with me because I was the only person you had to talk to. I'm different from what you're used to, Marlie. Maybe what you feel is curiosity."

"Why are you doing this?" she demanded, frustrated with his stubbornness.

"I'm trying to help you see things clearly."

"*I* see them clearly. It's you who doesn't. What do you feel for me, Cord? Tell me what you feel."

Cord remained silent.

Marlie threw herself against him, burying her head against his chest, sharing his heartbeat, soaking up his warmth. She couldn't let him slip away from her again. Not again! She reached out to wrap her arms around his midsection and in the process felt the bandage on his side.

Drawing a quick breath, she pulled back in concern.

"It's not bad," he said gruffly. "I've had worse."

Her fingers trembled as she ran them over his side. When she looked up at him, tears were swimming in her eyes. "You think what I feel for you isn't real. That it's something that will go away if you do. Well, that's not true, Cord. I know we haven't known each other long, and that the circumstances have been odd. But I'm not stupid." She took a halting breath. "I think you love me. You may not realize it yet, but one day you will. Why else did you stay? You didn't stay for the money, you weren't going to get more. You saved my life, my father's life—you didn't have to do either.

"You try to present yourself as being hard. I know you are; I know you've had to be to survive. But you're not as hard as you think you are, otherwise what happened in Africa wouldn't have bothered you and you wouldn't be wanting to quit. There's another side to you, Cord, a softer side. I see that in you even if you don't want me to.

"I love you," she continued. "I love you for your faults, for your weaknesses, even as I love you for your strengths. Nothing will change that. Not ever."

When she finished speaking, silence stretched between them. In it, Cord reached for her hand. Marlie allowed him to take it. She had opened her soul to his view.

He tried to speak, but he had to clear his throat before he could begin. "I don't know what to say, Marlie. I think what you've told me is an honor—" There was another stretch of silence. "But things can't work out between us. We're too different. We have different backgrounds, different upbringings, different scars—or no scars—from the way life has treated us."

"I don't care about that," Marlie protested. "I've never cared about that. It's you I love, Cord. Don't you see?"

Cord hesitated. He had never received such a profession before. Love and caring had been scarce commodities through most of his life. He smoothed her hair. How often at the safe house had he wanted to do that very thing? Run his fingers through the

wheat gold of her hair... Be able to kiss her at will...
To hold her... To make love to her... He had fought
his emotions, but they had remained in the back of his
consciousness, never giving him rest.

"I still think we should take some time, Marlie. I—
I want to wrap things up in my mind. And you should,
too. I don't want to destroy your life and that might
happen if we act too soon."

Again Marlie wanted to protest. But this time she
held her tongue. Nothing would change for her. She
would always love him. And if letting go—having
enough confidence to trust her love and to trust that
he would soon discover his love for her—meant that
much to him, she would do it.

"All right," she quietly agreed. "We'll wait. Only
where will you go? Not back to—"

Cord broke into her words. "No. Even if I'd never
met you, I think I was through with that line of work."

"What will you do?" She couldn't keep the concern from her voice.

"I have a friend in Louisiana. He's invited me to
visit. I think I might take him up on his offer."

"Where in Louisiana?"

"Near Morgan City."

"That's not too far away."

"I know."

"How—how long will it...?"

"I can't answer that, Marlie."

She suffered the answer. Her voice was tight when
she asked, "Will you come back to Houston occasionally?"

"No."

"Could I come to see you?" she tried again, giving him a brave smile.

The muscles of Cord's jaw clenched. "No. If we're going to give ourselves time, we can't complicate things by being together. It would be too—"

Marlie interrupted his denial by standing on tiptoe to kiss the strong line of his jaw that he held so firmly. "But what if I want to come?" she whispered huskily. Her soft lips moved over his throat while her body melted into his. If he was going to insist upon going away, she would give him something to think about while he was gone.

It was everything Cord could do to keep himself from tossing her onto the bed, but somehow he contained himself. Their bodies might be clamoring for the same thing, but that was a step they couldn't take. It wouldn't be right for her or for him. He couldn't make love and then leave. To make love to her equaled commitment.

When they separated, each looked steadily at the other.

"I suppose I should leave now," Marlie whispered, not feeling that she had enough strength left to put action to her words.

"Yes." The word was clipped.

She touched his hand, not wanting to go. "Will I see you again before you leave?"

"I don't think that would be a good idea."

"Will you call?"

"I'll try," Cord promised, but he wasn't sure that he would; the pain might be too great.

"I'll be waiting," she said softly. Then she broke all contact and moved to the door. On the way, she passed the bed. Would another man have given in? She knew that he wanted her just as much as she wanted him. But Cord was a different breed. He could deny himself if he thought an action would cause further complications. He refused to take advantage of her.

Integrity...a code for living. It beat so strongly in his soul and he barely knew that he possessed the trait. So much had happened to make him question himself. But she knew that it was there. She had recognized it in him from the beginning. It was one of the things she loved about him, respected in him.

Marlie paused at the door to glance back across the room. No longer were his features carved from stone. He looked very much a human being who was wrestling with a mass of conflicting desires.

She smiled softly, confidently. "Nothing will change my mind, Cord. I love you."

He made no reply. He couldn't. Emotion gripped his throat. One part of him applauded his sanity. Another part screamed at him not to let her go, to take what was offered and to hell with what followed. But he listened to his better side, which was something he would have to learn to do a lot more of in the future.

The door closed. He was alone in the room. He didn't move for many minutes.

Chapter Fifteen

R.J. sat in a rocking chair on the long porch that stretched across the rear of his house. A tiny desultory motion kept the chair in motion, rocking back and forth, one wooden leg creaking as it moved. Knife in hand, R.J. was whittling on a bar of soap, a habit he'd had since childhood. Under his skilled fingers, a king's knight was taking shape.

Periodically his gaze would lift to follow the man who was pacing restlessly from one section of the porch to another.

"It's a hot enough day without that," he finally said. "Why don't you sit down and cool off?"

Cord glanced at his friend. He had been here for three weeks and the inactivity was driving him mad. No, he contradicted himself. It wasn't inactivity. It was something in him, something he had to settle.

He tried to smile. "I don't know how you do it. Nothing ever happens here."

R.J. grinned. "I know. Isn't it wonderful?"

Cord took a seat on the first step, letting his long legs stretch across the ones below. He looked out over the slow-moving bayou, where a pair of cypress trees gave shade. Birds played among the many knees that jutted from the water.

Cord picked up a small stick and twirled it between his forefinger and thumb. "Don't you ever get bored?"

"Not usually. But then I'm not pining after some girl."

Cord met his friend's gaze. "What makes you think I am?"

R.J. put the chessman aside and stood up, stretching his frame before moving to stand close to the younger man. "It's not exactly hard to spot: restless, no appetite, very little sleep at night. Why don't you go back to Houston and get her? She's willing, isn't she?"

"I never told you that."

"Put it down to intuition again."

"Yeah, she's willing."

"Then what's stopping you?"

Cord threw the stick into the water and disturbed the birds. They flew off with squawks of protest and a flurry of wings.

"Every damn thing."

"Looks to me like it's only you who's stopping you."

"It's not as simple as it seems, R.J."

"I didn't think it was."

Cord ran a hand through his dark hair. "She's rich, for one thing."

"She can't help that."

"And she's innocent."

"You could take care of that in a half hour."

"I don't mean that way—although I think she is. It's... I'm not right for her. You know the kind of life I've led."

R.J. nodded, his mind going back over his many years.

"Things change you," Cord mused.

"They do. But not always for the worse." R.J. grunted as he, too, perched on the top stair. "I suppose it comes down to how much you love her."

Cord made no reply.

"I know if you look at this face of mine, you wouldn't think some girl could love me. But one did once."

"What happened to her?" Cord asked after a space of time had elapsed.

R.J. shrugged. "I don't know. The last I heard she was thinking about marrying an I.R.S. agent and settling down. They're probably busy raising lots of little I.R.S. grandchildren by now. Probably the most stupid thing I ever did in my life was walk out on her."

"I thought you were happy as you are."

"Oh, I am. It's just sometimes at night, when I'm lying in bed and the house is quiet, I wonder what might have happened *if*."

Cord stood up. "Well, I'm not going to wonder."

"You're going after her?"

"No."

R.J. screwed his eyes into slits.

Cord felt their wordless questioning. He shifted restively. "I'm just not going to think about her, that's all."

"Has it worked so far?"

The question hit Cord with devastating force. He turned away as if physically pushed.

R.J. said nothing more. Neither did Cord. In a few minutes he resumed his pacing while R.J. retrieved his knife and soap to finish the sculpture he had started.

CORD LAY ON HIS LONELY BED, as restless on it as a tortured monk. All he could think of was Marlie. It was almost as if she were an obsession. He never found rest—he hadn't since leaving Houston. And the quiet, uneventful days on the bayou didn't help. Maybe if he had something to do.

It wouldn't matter. She was a part of him. If he exorcised her, he would cast off a part of himself.

His arm came up to block the light of the moon, its weight resting across his eyes.

Marlie said she loved him. But what did she know of love? For that matter, what did he? From his earliest years he had witnessed little affection between his parents. And what had passed as love on the road, in quick furtive matings, taught nothing.

He had seen men die to protect others; he had seen mothers thrusting their children behind them, using their bodies as shields. But such a deep emotion had never touched him before. How did he know that what he felt for her was real? He had nothing to base it upon, except . . .

If she died, he died. It was as simple as that. Her life, her welfare meant more to him than his own.

Unconsciously, Cord's hand clenched into a fist. It was torture making himself stay away.

His mind skipped to what R.J. had told him. He didn't think he could stand it if he ever learned that

Marlie had fallen in love with someone else. It would kill him.

If only he could go to her cleansed of all the horror of his past. She said what had happened then didn't matter to her, but it mattered to him. So much of his life had been wasted. Was there anything left to redeem?

She loved him—at least she said that she did. And he wanted to believe her. She must have seen something in him.

Cord tossed restlessly for the next few hours, battling with his conscience, battling with the nearly irresistible urge to get into the van and drive to Houston. When he finally drifted into sleep, the miles that separated him from Marlie magically disappeared, along with all the strictures that kept them apart.

To the rest of the world, Marlie had not changed. Inside herself, she knew that she had.

Her father had come home from the hospital two weeks before and was now mending steadily, almost back to his old self. He never brought up Cord's name, as if not mentioning him would allow her to forget. But Marlie knew she never would. With each day that passed she became more sure of herself, of her aims, of what she wanted from life. There was no possibility that she still was influenced by what had occurred during that terrible time.

Regina noticed the change in her. But they were so close, Marlie wasn't surprised.

"He's a very lucky man," Regina said as they sat in the garden one evening, enjoying the lessening heat of day. She had just gotten back from a family vacation in Mexico and now looked all tanned and relaxed.

At first Marlie thought she was referring to her father. "Yes, he is. The doctor said a little more to either side and the bullet would have done a lot more damage."

"Well, that's true. You're father *is* lucky. But I meant someone else."

Marlie smiled slowly, understanding at last. "You got to meet him, didn't you?"

"I wouldn't exactly call it meeting. I was in my robe and he was shot. But I saw him, yes."

"He's quite something, isn't he?"

"I would say he is."

"He's special, Regina."

"Oh, I realize that . . . for you to love him."

"And I do. I really do."

"Does he love you?"

Marlie's eyes clouded. "I'm sure he does."

"But he's never told you?"

"No."

Regina frowned. "Where is he, then? I haven't gone selectively blind since I got back, have I?"

"He's— We're giving each other some time. He had some things to take care of and I guess I did, too. He's in Louisiana."

"I'm not sure I understand."

Marlie took a breath. "He thinks he's not good enough for me and that if we wait, I'll see that and go away."

"How ridiculous . . . He *is* good enough for you, isn't he?"

Marlie's mood lightened somewhat at her friend's quick question. "Of course. I told you, he's special."

"What will your father think?"

"He'll get used to the idea."

Regina smiled. "If he's wise he will, and he's always struck me as being wise. What about the man who shot him? Is he in jail, or what?"

"Dad's helping him as best he can. The man has mental problems. I think he's probably going to end up in treatment."

"Probably another wise idea. Ah, when are you and Cord...?"

Marlie looked into the distance. Her confidence was still there. She knew Cord loved her. But so many days had passed without a word from him. "Whenever he's ready."

Regina said nothing, but she read her friend's expression. Marlie wasn't as sure of Cord as she pretended—at least, she wasn't sure if he would return.

Regina glanced down at her clasped hands. She hoped her friend wouldn't be hurt too badly. To help divert her attention to another subject she said, "I took your advice."

"I gave you advice?"

Regina nodded. "About my mother. While we were away, I found a quiet moment when it was just the two of us and I knew we wouldn't be interrupted. We talked. I did it exactly as you said—not laying any blame, just talking woman-to-woman. And you know, she understood. She didn't realize how she was treating me. Oh, everything's not going to change completely. It's her nature to nurture, but things are better already and when she starts hovering too much, I remind her and we laugh."

"I don't think I had all that much to do with it. It was the two of you. All you needed was a nudge."

"What's this about a nudge? Is my daughter telling tales behind my back?" Unknown to Marlie and Regina, William had stepped through the French doors into the patio. He was still pale and a bit weak at times, but he had insisted upon going into the office that morning, for a limited amount of time at first.

Marlie and Regina laughed, as he wanted them to.

William looked at his daughter. "Telephone, honey."

Marlie instantly got to her feet. "Who is it?" she asked quickly, breathlessly, just as she had each time over the past weeks when she received a call.

"Mrs. Cohen, I believe. Something about a raffle."

"Oh." Marlie tried not to let her disappointment show, but as time passed, she was having more difficulty. "Okay, thanks. I'll just..."

After she moved into the house, William took her chair. His gaze held a certain sadness as he glanced at Regina.

"I'm worried about her," he said quietly.

Regina nodded. "She loves him."

"I know."

"Do you object?"

"I'm not sure. I want her to be happy."

"And she might not be with him?"

William shrugged.

"I only met him for a few minutes, under rather difficult circumstances, but he impressed me," Regina said.

"Yes," William agreed, "he's impressive."

"But . . . ?"

"But I don't think he's right for her."

"He seems to think that, too."

"He does?" William was surprised.

"That's what Marlie says. You haven't talked with her?"

"Not about him. I was hoping she might forget him."

"I wouldn't count on that, if I were you. I don't think she will."

"I wish none of this had happened," William muttered intensely.

Regina was silent a moment then, impulsively, she reached out to touch William's arm. "Marlie's a grown woman. She makes decisions on her own. You can't control her life. If she's going to be hurt, she will be. There's nothing you can do about it. There's nothing either of us can do about it, except be there if she needs us."

William was startled by Regina's words. In all the years he had known her, watching her grow from childhood with Marlie, this was the first time she had not acted awed by him. He knew that what she said made sense. Marlie was an adult, her life was her own. But he couldn't help being afraid for her.

"Yes," he said. He patted Regina's hand. In their concern, they were united.

THE HOUSE WAS QUIET as Marlie moved through it. She had no idea what time it was, except morning was still some hours away. She had been asleep, but then like so many nights recently, her sleep had been broken and after tossing and turning for some time, she had finally gotten up.

Her father was sleeping peacefully; she heard his soft snores as she passed his room. She moved down the stairway with no destination in mind, but she knew she couldn't stay upstairs any longer. She felt confined, trapped. Within her room, within her emotions.

She stepped through the French doors into the garden, breathing deeply of the cool, moist air that was scented with a delicate rose perfume. The full moon lighted her way as she moved into the night. And a short distance away, a tree frog chirped for rain even though the ground was still damp from the latest shower.

In fact, droplets of rain were still pooling on the tree leaves and as she walked, some dripped on her, dampening her hair, her face, the light wrap that she wore. She turned her face upward, enjoying the sensation.

But as she opened her eyes, tears mixed with the coolness of the raindrops. She had wanted to cry for days, but hadn't allowed herself. Now, completely alone, she was unable to stop.

Would Cord come back for her? Would he listen to his heart and not his mind, and take that final step that would allow them both to have a full life?

She missed him and she was afraid—

She wrapped her arms closely around herself, holding tightly. Her body ached to feel him near, to hear his voice, to see his face. If anything, her love for him had increased.

What if he didn't come? She might have to face that fact one day. What would she do? Would she try to find him, try to force him... But love couldn't be forced; neither could commitment.

A fresh spate of tears rushed into her eyes. She would die if he didn't come. Maybe not physically, but something in her would never be the same.

Moisture collected and pooled, then it escaped. She didn't try to wipe her tears away. There was no one to see.

A bush rustled softly nearby, but Marlie paid it no heed. She was too miserable to pay attention to prowling cats or dogs. Waiting was so hard.

She moved farther down the path, her steps slow, almost painful. She touched a creamy rose petal whose color was muted in the light. She bent to sniff it.

Then she stiffened, her body alert before her mind. There had been a sound. She was not alone in the garden. Remembered fear caused her to spin around.

A tall form slowly emerged from the darkness beneath the trees. She caught her breath, her heart pumping erratically.

The form moved upon her like a jungle cat, its feet not making a sound, its body gliding, on the hunt.

She gave a small gasp.

The figure stopped several feet away from her. Now she could see his face in the moonlight, see the expression in his eyes... and she was afraid to move, afraid that he might be an apparition, something her mind had conjured.

Then he spoke. "Don't cry, Marlie."

Marlie murmured something incoherent.

Cord lifted his arms to her and without hesitating any longer, she threw herself across the distance that separated them.

She hit him with force, but he was barely aware of it. He had been watching her for some time, ever since she left the house. Before that, he had been watching her room, trying to content himself with the knowledge that she was near.

Her body trembled against him; her tears were dampening the material of his shirt. She was making small soft sounds, forming more words that he could not understand. But it didn't matter. Nothing mattered except that she was in his arms.

Marlie buried herself against him, clutching him, not wanting to wake up if this was a dream. Her hands moved over him, trying to assure herself that he was real.

Then he was pushing her away, but only enough so that he could cup her face in his hands. He looked down at her, at the blueness of her eyes that was intensified by their dampness, at the sweetness of her face that was reaching out to his heart.

He murmured her name, then he could restrain himself no longer. His mouth swooped down to cover hers in a kiss that held nothing back. He loved her. Whatever she wanted, he wanted, and if she wanted to blend their lives, to take the chance...

Marlie kissed him back with all the longing of past days adding to her passionate response.

One kiss turned into many. Finally, breathless, he brought her head to his chest, holding her there, needing to feel her near even as he tried to gain a measure of control.

Marlie clung to him, laughing softly, incredulously. He was here! He had come! All those days of torture had paid off.

When she could, she whispered, "I was afraid you wouldn't come."

In those short words, Cord could hear the pain she had suffered. His heart ached for her, but he had suffered as well.

"I'm here," he said shakily.

"Yes," she murmured, burrowing even closer against his chest.

"I couldn't stay away."

"Good."

Cord lifted her chin and kissed her again. This time with more care, giving each of them time to fully appreciate the other.

When they broke apart, Marlie continued to look at him. "You'll stay?" she asked. She held her breath for his answer. Maybe he hadn't decided yet. Maybe this was just an aberration.

"If you'll have me."

She began to smile and the glow of love in her eyes was almost more than he could bear to see. He still didn't think that he deserved her, but he had no life without her.

"I'll have you," she breathed. "Cord, if it's possible, I love you more now than I did before. Being away from you has only—"

"I almost went mad in Louisiana. I wouldn't let myself— I tried to stay away." He swallowed. "I love you, Marlie. I tried to fight it . . ."

"Don't!" she whispered fiercely. "I told you before that I don't care about your past. You are what you are because of it. I don't want to change you."

"I want to change myself."

"Then we'll change together. But don't ever leave me again, Cord. I don't think I could take it."

His hands came out to cup her face again. He touched her with infinite gentleness. "I never thought I'd ever say these words—especially to you," he mused softly, "but, Marlie, will you marry me? I can't promise you the kind of life that you have now. I can't promise you anything. I don't know what I'm going to do, how I'm going to provide for you. But if you're willing to take the chance . . ."

Marlie was scarcely able to believe what was happening. Such a short time before, she was so caught up in misery.

"Marrying you isn't taking a chance, Cord. I'll marry you. And it won't be a mistake. We won't *let* it be a mistake."

"No," he murmured in agreement. Then he dipped his head, putting his lips to hers, giving and receiving a wondrous kiss that would forever seal the bond between them.

The scrap of paper they would receive upon their marriage meant nothing to Cord. Official papers had their place, but the vow he was making in his heart at this moment was what counted to him.

He would honor Marlie, protect her, for the rest of his life.

Nothing else mattered.

Marlie sensed the importance of the moment. Once Cord gave his word, it was there for eternity. Never again would she have to question his commitment to her.

With all her might she tried to show him that she felt the same.

Chapter Sixteen

The darkness just before sunrise found Marlie and Cord sitting together in one of the big chairs in her father's study. She was in his lap, her head resting on his shoulder and tucked snugly against his cheek. His arms were around her just as hers were around him. They had been there since coming in from the garden a short time before.

When they had first entered the room, Cord's memories of the last time he had seen it caused him to flinch. He had come so close to losing Marlie, and then her father had been badly wounded. She had seen his dismay and guided his thoughts away from that time by kissing him. Moments later, they had sunk into the chair and it was there that they had remained.

"My father is nearly well now. He even went to the office yesterday for a couple of hours," Marlie said, resting her head against his shoulder.

"When he hears about us, he'll probably have a relapse," Cord murmured dryly.

She grinned. "I don't think so."

"How do you think he'll react?"

"He already knows I love you."

"You told him?"

Marlie nodded. "When he was in the hospital. Before you left for Louisiana. How else do you think I found you?"

"He helped?" Cord asked, amazed.

Again Marlie nodded.

"But this . . . this is a little more than helping you to find me."

"He'll get used to it."

"He doesn't like me."

"He doesn't know you."

"He knew me enough to hire me to protect you," Cord reminded her.

"Did he pay you a lot?" Marlie asked curiously.

"Enough. Enough to help us get started, I think."

"Doing what?"

"I'm not sure. Maybe what you said back at the safe house. From the quality of the men he hired to protect you, Houston could certainly use a good security consulting firm. Maybe I could even convince R.J. to come into it with me, though I doubt it."

"Who's R.J.?"

"My friend from Louisiana. He, ah, retired from the same line of work that I did."

"I'd like to meet him sometime."

"We'll try to arrange that."

Marlie shifted position. She moved her fingers over his shirt, causing him to stir in reaction. She thrilled to the idea that she could disturb him so easily, but, then, he could do the same to her.

"Cord?"

"Hmm?"

"Will you be bored? I mean—" She rushed on when she felt him start to speak. "You're accustomed to so much freedom...and a lot of...things going on."

"Too many things went on," he cut in swiftly.

At that moment the door to the room opened and William strode in. He visibly started when he realized that the room was not empty, then he blanched, his skin lightening to such a degree that Marlie jumped from Cord's lap to assist him.

"Dad?" she cried, reaching for his arm. He stood as still as stone.

William's eyes were riveted on Cord. "You," he said weakly.

Cord slowly rose to his feet. "Mr. Richards."

Her father's gaze moved to Marlie. He didn't say anything but she knew the question he was asking. She held her hand out to Cord, silently asking him to come to her. He did as she requested.

"Dad," she said softly. "Cord's asked me to marry him. I said yes."

William suddenly became cold all over. He hadn't wanted to hear those words, but he knew from the instant that he saw them together that they would come.

He was at a momentary loss. He didn't know what to say. Then, as the seconds passed, he realized that there was very little he could say. If Cord Anderson was Marlie's choice, it was not for him to stand in the way. But he didn't want to give her up yet. Not yet. She was still so young.

Cord read William's face. He could see the struggle going on inside the man. "I'll take care of her, sir," he said quietly, "with my life."

William looked steadily at Cord. He remembered the day the younger man had first come into his office. He had been such an enigma then—he still was, in many respects. But he had saved Marlie's life, even after being summarily dismissed, and that was something William could never repay.

What he knew of Cord's history was not reassuring. He was a hard man, one accustomed to hard choices. William was sure there were instances that, if stated, would horrify both Marlie and himself. But the past belonged in the past, and mistakes were there to be learned from. It wasn't as if he hadn't made mistakes of his own. He had. And it was one of his own that had brought Cord Anderson into Marlie's life.

After a moment, Cord extended his hand.

When William took it, Marlie gave an inarticulate cry and hugged them both with delight.

ONE WEEK LATER Marlie and Cord were married. It was a small ceremony, performed by a judge who was a friend of Marlie's father. Regina and her family were there, along with R.J., who had driven in from Morgan City for the day. Marlie had liked him at first sight, and the feeling seemed to be mutual. Even William had responded to the man's determined humor. R.J. had acted the wicked leprechaun, teasing Cord, teasing Marlie, teasing William. But Marlie sensed another side to him and when he pulled her aside at the small reception at her home, and whispered seriously in her ear, she listened to him.

"Cord will make you a good husband. Don't you ever worry about that. He's had some hard knocks, but so have we all. If he ever gets ornery, just send him to me and I'll whip him back into shape."

"I'll remember that," she assured him, a twinkle in her eye.

Cord stepped close to them, putting an arm protectively around Marlie's shoulders. "What are you telling her, R.J.?"

"Just that I'll whip you into shape if you ever give her a moment's worry. That's all."

"Oh?"

"And I told him I'd remember that," Marlie confirmed.

Cord gazed at his wife's smiling face. "What about me? Who do I send you to if you get out of line?"

"My father?" she suggested.

Cord laughed.

He looked so handsome, Marlie thought. She had never seen him in a suit before and the experience was definitely devastating. She clung to his side, not ever wanting to be parted from him.

"Your father would probably take your side. That wouldn't do me any good."

Marlie glanced at her father, who was talking with the Campos. He had been relatively quiet throughout the short ceremony and after they had arrived home as well. She knew he was a bit upset by what was happening. She wished that she could do something to make everything better for him. But she couldn't give up Cord. Her father would soon see that, even if he couldn't now.

Cord followed her gaze. "We can postpone the honeymoon, if you like," he said softly. "Mexico will still be there in a couple of weeks."

Marlie squeezed his hand, loving him all the more for his sensitivity to her father.

"Maybe if I talk to him," she ventured.

Cord shook his head. "No. I think maybe that's something I need to do."

He loosened his hold on Marlie and set his shoulders. The walk across the room was long. He and William had spoken very little during that week. At least, not about anything important.

He stepped close to the other man and murmured, "Why don't we take a little walk."

William looked momentarily surprised and then agreed. He excused himself to the Campos before turning to follow Cord.

Cord stepped into the garden, breathing the fragrant air, preparing himself for what was to come.

William fell into step at his side.

Cord drew another breath and started, not giving the other man a chance to speak first. "I know you think Marlie could have done better. I do, too. But she didn't. She chose me. And I'm going to do my damnedest to see that she never regrets it." He paused. "Now, we'd like to live in Houston—Marlie's roots are here and I'm thinking of starting a business—but if you're going to give us nothing but misery, we're leaving. Do you understand?"

William was silent but he continued to walk at Cord's side.

"I understand," he said at last. "And I agree."

Now it was Cord's turn to be silent. Finally he said, "Just so we understand each other."

The path they were on led them back to the house. Marlie was standing in the doorway.

"Is everything all right?" she asked anxiously.

"Everything's fine," her father replied.

"Fine," Cord concurred.

Marlie looked from one to the other. She wasn't totally convinced, but she knew that neither of them would lie to her. Hooking her arms through theirs, they returned to the living room together.

Marlie threw her bouquet and Regina, being the only single woman present, had a clear field at catching it. Her friend's eyes were shining with happiness when she hugged Marlie close as the newlyweds prepared to leave.

"I'll keep an eye on your dad, Marlie," she whispered. "Don't worry about him."

Marlie nodded, unable to say anything. Regina was such a good friend. She could never be replaced.

When she straightened, it was to face her father. He looked at her for a moment before gathering her into his arms. Cord stood close by, watching.

"I want you to be happy, honey," William said, his voice husky. "That's all I've ever wanted for you." He turned to his new son-in-law and extended his hand. "You didn't need to say what you did in the garden just now. When you have a daughter of your own one day, maybe then you'll understand how I feel. Until then..." The two men clasped hands in the age-old ceremony. "Until then, welcome to the family, Cord."

Cord's throat tightened. He could see the sincerity in William Richards's eyes.

Epilogue

Marlie stretched, arching her body. When she encountered the sleeping form of her husband, she smiled softly to herself, partly in the remaining vestiges of sleep, partly in contentment. She turned to snuggle against him, making her body fit the curved line of his.

It was still hard for her to believe that this was real. She had been his wife for three days and they were three of the happiest days of her life.

Cord stirred, called from sleep by her touch. When he looked at her, she smiled and lifted a finger to trace the tiny scar that marked one section of his chest. She was coming to know his body, just as he was coming to know hers. He had many scars in many places, evidence of the difficult and dangerous life he had led. But none of them took away from his beauty—a long, lean body with muscles well-honed from use.

He caught her hand and raised it to his lips. "Good morning, Mrs. Anderson," he murmured.

"Good morning to you, Mr. Anderson," she returned.

"Would you mind telling me how you manage to get more beautiful each morning?"

"It's a secret I promised never to tell."

"And without makeup yet."

"You had fair warning. I never wore makeup at the safe house. I didn't have any."

"I remember. You looked like you were about fifteen. But then, you weren't exactly what I expected in any other way, either."

Marlie leaned on her elbow. "What were you expecting?"

"A spoiled, sophisticated woman."

"Which I'm not."

"Which you're not. But I soon began to wish that you were. It would have made my job easier. Then I could have ignored you."

Marlie smiled, pleased. "You had a hard time ignoring me?"

"What do you think?" he returned sardonically. "You began to get to me from the first. Always asking questions, always trying to get me to talk."

"You interested me."

"Why?"

"Because you were so different. And because I suspected that there was more to you than you wanted people to see."

"Did you find out more than you wanted to know?"

"No."

Cord played with her fingers, lacing his in and out.

"I don't have those dreams anymore," he murmured.

"Maybe they'll never come back."

He shrugged. "Who knows? But if they do, I'll have you to help me get through them." His eyes met hers.

Marlie held his gaze steadily. "You'll always have me," she said.

Cord made no reply.

Voices sounded from outside their cabana. For some time, other residents of the nearby huts had been awakening, ready to enjoy their day on the beautiful white Mexican sands and in the clear blue waters. A mother was scolding her child; the child was screaming a protest.

But the noise did not divert Cord's attention from his wife. For him, the rest of the world had retreated, a world that too often had shown him only ugliness and horror and uncomfortable reality. Now there was only Marlie. And in her hands, resting in their gentleness and in their care, was his heart.

Silhouette Sensation

A marvellous new series from Silhouette!

FEBRUARY TITLES

Silhouette Sensation

COMING NEXT MONTH

LEGACY
Maura Seger

Gwen Llywelyn came to Myrddin's Rock to sell the ancient Welsh castle that one branch of her family had called home for generations, but she found that she couldn't deny her heritage.

Owen Garrett taught her the magic of the past while protecting her from the danger of the present. But Owen wasn't all he seemed, and soon Gwen had to ask: should she really be dreaming of a shared future?

BRIDE OF THE TIGER
Heather Graham Pozzessere

When Tara first saw Rafe Tyler she thought that he belonged in the jungle; he reminded her of a tiger stalking its prey. When he followed her, she realised she was right. He was a hunter, and he was hunting her.

Rafe would do whatever was necessary to find out what really happened to his stepbrother. He was certain that Tara Hill knew the truth. Once he'd met her, he knew he wanted far more than information from Tara.

Take 4 NEW Silhouette Sensations FREE!

Silhouette **Sensation** is a thrilling NEW Silhouette series for the woman of today. Each tale is a full 256 pages long - a beautiful blend of sensitivity and sensuality. When you've enjoyed your FREE **Sensations** there's an extra treat in store!

You could go on to enjoy four more exciting new **Sensations**, delivered to your door each month - at just £1.35 each *(we pay postage & packing)*. **Plus** a **FREE** newsletter and lots more!

No strings attached - you can stop receiving books at any time.

EXTRA FREE GIFT
If you reply within 10 days

Post the coupon **NOW** and we'll send you this beautiful Digital Quartz Clock **plus** a surprise mystery gift!
